SHATTERED REIGN

BRENTSON UNIVERSITY SERIES
BOOK 6

BRI BLACKWOOD

BRETAGEY PRESS

Copyright © 2023 by Bri Blackwood

This is a work of fiction. Names, characters, places, and incidents either are the product of the author's imagination or are used fictitiously. Any resemblance to actual persons, living or dead, events, or locales is entirely coincidental. For more information, contact Bri Blackwood.

No part of this book may be reproduced in any form or by any electronic or mechanical means, including information storage and retrieval systems, without written permission from the author, except for the use of brief quotations in a book review.

The subject matter is not appropriate for minors. Please note this novel contains sexual situations, violence, sensitive and offensive language, and dark themes. It also has situations that are dubious and could be triggering.

First Digital Edition: August 2023

Cover Designed by Amanda Walker PA and Design

Edited by: Chrisandra Corrections

Fairy Proofmother Proofreading

EAL Editing Services

 Created with Vellum

NOTE FROM THE AUTHOR

Hello!

Thank you for taking the time to read this book. Shattered Reign is a dark college billionaire brother's best friend enemies-to-lovers romance. It is not recommended for minors and contains situations that are dubious and could be triggering. The book also includes stalking and graphic violence. It isn't a standalone and the book ends in an HEA for this couple. This series is complete.

Please note that this world is interconnected with The Lies Beneath/ The Westwick University Series and that chapter 29 in this book ends on a cliffhanger for that series.

BLURB

It was my turn...

I set my life ablaze,

And left everything I knew behind.

It was the first time in forever that I'd felt safe.

Safe from other people's expectations.

Safe from the person who was following my every move.

But I was far away from the one I loved the most.

It was a sacrifice I needed to make to keep myself safe.

...Until protecting myself was no longer an option.

PLAYLIST

Castles Crumbling — Taylor Swift, Hayley Williams
Always Remember Us This Way — Lady Gaga
My Blood — Ellie Goulding
Chasing Cars — Snow Patrol
If You're Not The One — Daniel Bedingfield
Thinking Out Loud — Ed Sheeran
Adore You — Harry Styles
Something Just Like This — The Chainsmokers, Coldplay
Counting Stars — One Republic
Unwritten — Natasha Bedingfield

The playlist can be found on Spotify.

1

BIANCA

y breath was caught in my throat as I watched out the window as the plane descended toward the tarmac. I was more than happy to leave my troubles behind in the United States, and I couldn't wait to escape to the Amalfi Coast in Italy.

But first, I needed to land in Naples.

A rush of air left my lungs as I felt the gentle jostle of the wheels of the plane making contact with solid ground. I gripped my seat's armrest hard as though the sudden contact would send me spiraling back to the chaos I was trying to leave behind. Was my reaction overkill? Sure, but I still did it anyway.

The plane taxied along the runway, and when we finally came to a stop, I inhaled and exhaled. It was the first breath I'd taken that didn't feel as if I had a heavy weight on my chest. I took out my compact mirror and opened it up. I double-checked my face before packing away my things and saw the dark circles that had landed under my eyes were still there.

Shit.

Tiffany, the flight attendant on this flight, walked up to me with a bright smile on her face. "It was lovely having you on this flight, Miss Henson."

"Thank you," I replied. "I appreciate, well, all of this."

And I did.

I gathered the things I'd brought with me on the plane, including the two phones I now had, and pulled my sunglasses down over my eyes. Sleeping on the plane had been okay, surprisingly, but I wasn't prepared to take on the brightness of the sun.

When I stepped off the plane and made it through customs, there was a town car waiting for me outside of the airport. The sleek black vehicle and its driver promised to bring me to what would become my home for the time being. The driver offered a polite nod as he took my luggage and placed it in the trunk. He then opened the door for me and waited until I was situated in the car before closing the door behind me. As he slid into the driver's seat and started the car, he didn't try to start a conversation with me, and I was more than happy with the silence that surrounded us.

As we pulled away from the airport, I glanced back as it grew smaller the farther we drove away from it. It was surreal, leaving everything behind, going off to a different country, let alone a different continent, but I couldn't deny that I felt freer here. I quickly did some research on my phone and saw that our drive to the Amalfi Coast would be about an hour, and I knew it was my chance for a fresh start of sorts.

The idea that anyone would recognize me here almost didn't exist. If this became a bigger story, there was a chance that they might recognize my father's face but not mine. This was the perfect opportunity for me to reinvent myself. I was no longer the daughter of a United States mayor who aspired for higher office. Now I was simply an American tourist who decided to vacation in Italy. And I was prepared to embrace every bit of that wholeheartedly.

My driver for the morning drove with the confidence of someone who'd done this drive a million times before. As we got closer to the coast, I was never left feeling unsafe as he navigated us along the roads to my destination. The winding roads would prove to be difficult for me without a doubt, so I was grateful to have someone that was way more experienced with this drive than I ever would be.

It also gave me the opportunity to take photos to remember all of this by. I snapped a few photos of the landscapes that I was able to see from the car and took a few minutes to view them on the phone. The picture was beautiful but did little to completely capture the beauty in real life.

As we made our way through the narrow streets, I couldn't help but notice how every corner seemed to contain a new surprise. A beautiful café here, a bustling market there. I was falling in love, and I'd only been here a couple of hours.

Once we arrived in Ravello, a town on the Amalfi Coast, my heart felt as if it was jumping in my body. I knew I was in the same town where my hotel was located, and it was only a matter of time before I arrived.

Then the driver put the car in park outside of a beautiful, statuesque building that was located on the cliffside.

This was it.

The place I would be staying at for... who knew how long. And I was okay with not knowing.

I pulled my coat tighter as a chill hit me. I couldn't help but wonder what everything would be like when it was summertime here. I couldn't wait to get a better look at the water from my room. Before I completely left the car that I had arrived in, I looked around, wondering if I was being followed by the person who decided stalking me was a good thing. Luckily for me, since the moment I'd shut off my old phone, I hadn't heard a thing from anyone, and that was exactly what I wanted.

As I walked into the hotel, I couldn't help but love the warm and inviting glow that surrounded me. The murals adorning the walls told stories of an era that was long gone, but between the arched ceilings, chandeliers, and furnishings, I was beginning to think that I'd been transported back in time.

I was greeted by a friendly-looking gentleman who stood near the front door of the hotel and hurried to grab my bags. I followed him up to the front desk, where a woman looked up from her computer and gave me a wide smile.

"Buongiorno. How may I help you?"

"I'm here to check in. My name is Bianca Henson."

Once she was able to find my reservation, she went through the usual check-in protocols. She also took the time to explain the amenities and services the hotel offered, which included an infinity pool with a breathtaking view of the sea, a spa, two restaurants, and a concierge service that would have no problem taking care of my every need.

After I was checked in and shown my room, I was blown away by it all. Although the amenities seemed to be contemporary, many elements in my room still looked to be from a different era.

As I walked to the balcony, I stared out at the ocean and coastline that were in front of me.

Here I was, in this luxurious suite, with this beautiful view. I felt at peace and for the first time in such a long while, I fully embraced that I'd made the right decision.

I couldn't get enough of this view, and I needed to take more photos of the scenery. I needed to take as many pictures as I could throughout my stay because there was no way that anyone back home would believe this.

Then again, who did I have to show this to back home?

My parents wouldn't have cared normally, but now even more so. As far as I knew, they didn't know I was the one who set into motion all the events that occurred over the last half a day or so, but I'm sure it would be red flag central that I wasn't at the party, and the fact that I wasn't answering my old phone.

Then again, that was if they were even attempting to call me. They might be too busy dealing with the shitstorm I created.

Well, the one that they'd started, and I now put an end to.

Although I'd had help in the form of a video leaking— which I really needed to find out how in the hell that happened—I was the reason for all of the dominos tumbling down. But if they hadn't tried to orchestrate a fake engagement and wedding, then none of this would have occurred. Or I wouldn't have been the cause of it all happening, at least.

My brother might be interested, but who knew how he was feeling since he might be in the direct line of fire due to the implosion of my father's political career.

Iris, my best friend, was who knew where and the guilt from having left her sat heavy in my stomach.

Then there was Easton. I didn't even want to begin to think of what might be going through his mind.

Instead, I grabbed my phone and began snapping photos of the landscape. Once I was done, I walked back into my suite and unpacked my things. After that, I decided that resting would do me a bit of good, given the journey I'd just been on. I probably should stay awake in order to try to fix my internal clock after the time zone change, but I couldn't make myself give a fuck. I decided to take a quick shower before putting on a pair of sweats, setting an alarm so I didn't sleep too long, and getting into bed.

The bed felt like heaven on earth, and I was ready to embrace the sleep that awaited me.

But first, my mind wandered back to what I thought might have happened after the news broke about my father's lies and infidelity.

2

EASTON

SEVERAL HOURS EARLIER

If you had told me that the world had come to a standstill, I would have believed you. The awkwardness that permeated every surface in this room was suffocating. I glanced over at Raven, and she looked as if she was ready to melt into Nash if she could have. I didn't blame her.

Shock was present on every face in the room as the breaking news that everyone had just read sank in. Murmurs picked up as the Hensons' guests couldn't believe what they were reading and experiencing. It was a chaotic scene without the physical signs of chaos.

What none of this gave me any insight into was where on earth Bianca was.

My eyes searched through the crowd, looking for her once more, but landed on her mother instead. Her face had turned pale, and based on her expression, I was beginning to wonder if she was going to faint. I watched as Mayor Henson walked up to her and tried to put his hand on her shoulder, but she wasn't having it.

She moved her body away from his and issued him a

strong glare as if to warn him not to try that move again. When Mayor Henson tried to whisper something in Mrs. Henson's ear, she threw her head back in disgust and walked away from him. It took him a couple of seconds to realize what had happened before he was soon following behind her.

I found Diana Caldwell standing with her mouth open and a hand over her chest in one of the corners of the room. Her reaction was over the top compared to everyone else's at the party. I still couldn't shake the feeling that she was somehow involved, even though I didn't have any definitive proof.

"I'm going to check on my parents," Nash said.

I was forced to look back at him because I couldn't believe the words that had come out of his mouth. After everything they'd done, he still felt the need to check on them.

"I'll go with you," Raven replied as she grabbed his hand. Together the couple walked away, leaving me to my own devices.

I was happy that he wouldn't be left alone to deal with the mess he was about to walk into. I wasn't sure if it had been my place to offer to go with him, given the recent troubles we'd had. This freed me up to do what I needed to do and find the only person that I really wanted to be around at this moment.

Bianca. Where the hell was she?

"Easton?"

I turned and found my parents standing near me. I'd been so distracted that I hadn't seen them approach. The look on their faces was what I suspected everyone here was feeling.

Shock. Concern. Confusion.

"Can you believe all of this? Do you think this is true?"

It took me half a second to process my mother's questions.

I swallowed hard and nodded. "Yes. The fact that he didn't try to deny it makes me think it's true. From what we've seen, Van is very good at putting on a brave face and has side-stepped other allegations in the time we've known him. He didn't try today."

My parents looked at each other in shock before turning their attention back to me.

"This is a disaster for everyone involved, but especially Mrs. Henson, Bianca, and Nash. We need to be there for them if they need us," my mother said with finality.

I agreed with her and wanted to make sure that I was there for Bianca especially. But she was still nowhere to be found.

"Yes. I wonder what it is that we can do." my father spoke this time, but I barely heard him.

My eyes landed on the only person left here that might be able to help me.

I eyed Tristan for a moment, the person who was supposed to be the man of the hour. Although he was reading something on his phone, I noticed how calm and collected he looked. Shouldn't he be reacting differently to his fiancée not showing up for their engagement party? Why doesn't he seem surprised or bothered by this news?

"Hey, I found someone I want to talk to for a moment. I'll be right back, okay?"

Both of my parents nodded, and I made my way across the room to the man I hoped held the key to all of this.

I cleared my throat as I approached him, and he looked up from his phone.

"Tristan," I said as my heartbeat pounded in my ears.

"Easton," he replied back, taking me slightly off guard.

"You know my name?" It seemed as if he knew more about me than I knew about him. I didn't like that at all.

"Your parents' reputation precedes them. Of course, I know who you are. Some might say it's my job to know who you are."

Part of me wanted to ask what he meant by that, but that would only delay me getting the answers I wanted.

"Where is Bianca?"

His smile faltered slightly, and I could feel him studying me. What he was searching for, I wasn't sure. "Why are you asking me?"

"Shouldn't you know where the person you're supposed to marry is?" I was already on edge, and I didn't feel like trading barbs back and forth with him.

"She's not here."

I clenched my jaw to stop myself from rolling my eyes. "That's obvious. Where is she?"

Instead of responding, he stared at me, and the look was unsettling, but it didn't deter me. His gaze bore into me, dissecting every nuance of my facial expression and posture. I could see the gears turning in his mind. It was as if he was trying to see my true motive without having to ask me.

I didn't have time for his games while Bianca was who knew where. "Do you know where she is? If not, you're just wasting my time."

"You love her."

My eyes widened because I hadn't been expecting that. He smirked in return, having caught my reaction. His statement hung in the air between us. He'd seen through my facade of indifference and straight to the worry and love I held for her. While I had been getting used to the fact that I loved her and had created a plan to stop this whole fake engagement, I hadn't admitted it to anyone. Hearing it out loud was jarring, to say the least.

Fuck.

"Seems as if I was right. It also explains some of her behavior too."

"What do you mean?"

Tristan put his phone back into his pocket and leaned in closer to me. "Bianca didn't come out and say it, but I suspected feelings for someone else might have been one of the reasons why she tried to get out of this arrangement."

I didn't have time to be going in circles with him. "Okay, but do you know where she is?"

He turned his wrist so that he could read his watch before he looked back at me. "She should be on a flight to the Amalfi Coast."

"Italy?" It wasn't that I didn't know where it was, but I couldn't believe that she would travel there.

"That's right. I can give you her exact location and everything." He pulled out his phone and started typing, but there was no way that he had my number because—

When my phone vibrated in my pocket, I narrowed my gaze at him and he raised an eyebrow at me, daring me to say something. I made sure that he gave me the name of her hotel before stuffing it back into my pocket.

"Thank you."

Tristan held out his hand, and as we shook, he said, "My pleasure. Her request was for me not to tell her parents if they asked."

Based on what I knew of them, I wondered if they would. "I have no intention of letting them know."

"Excellent. Take care of her, okay? I might not know her well, but I do know that she's special. And very brave."

I let his words hang in the air for a moment, agreeing with the nice things that he'd said about her. She was, without a doubt, all of that and more. And I had every intention of taking care of her, but I didn't say another word. I pulled my hand back instead and walked away, more determined than when I'd walked toward him. It took some slight maneuvering, but I found my parents standing in a different place in the room than where I'd left them.

"Mom, Dad," I said as I shifted my gaze between the two of them, making sure to lock eyes with both of them. I was aware that my next words would catch them by surprise, but I'd already made my decision. "It looks like I'm spending the holidays elsewhere this year."

The silence that followed stood between us like a heavy cloud. They exchanged a quick glance, using their eyes to speak a silent language that only they knew how to decipher.

"Is that right?" Mom asked, her tone indicating that she was shocked by my announcement. "Why don't you fill us in so we can see how we can help you achieve your end goal?"

Those were just the words I needed to hear.

3

BIANCA

PRESENT TIME

That evening, I stood on my balcony overlooking the Amalfi Coast once more just as the sun began to set. The sky was a beautiful mix of vibrant pinks and oranges, with slices of purple and blue around the clouds. Slightly below, or so it looked, the sea shimmered in the fading light, giving me an opportunity to take in its beauty before nightfall. Part of me wished that I was down there, walking along the beach, enjoying every ounce of this view.

While the air was still fresh and crisp, it had grown colder than it had been earlier. Yet, I still couldn't quite convince myself to move inside. I couldn't help but wish I'd grabbed something to put over my arms before I walked out here, but it wasn't enough to make me leave this spot.

Maybe it was due to the wineglass in my hand, filled with a deep-red liquid. The light danced off the edges of the glass and I couldn't help but look at it too. Ordering a bottle of wine from room service because I could had been an idea, but I wasn't completely sure it was a good one. I took a deep breath and brought the glass to my lips and hesitated. It was a temptation I couldn't resist, especially because I could legally drink it here.

As the liquid flowed down my throat, the slight burn led to my mind starting to calm and push aside my racing thoughts. With each sip, there was also a nagging feeling that I shouldn't be drinking. Deep down, I knew that I was playing with fire, yet I still put myself in this predicament.

I knew the delicate balance that existed between indulgence and going completely over the cliff, yet here I was, walking along a tightrope on the edge of temptation. I couldn't deny that I was enjoying the position I was in, even if it was dangerous.

I told myself this would be the only glass I would have tonight, but it was a slippery slope between one glass and several. I'd even said the promise out loud, but it was something that only me and the cool night air had heard. I was the only person who was going to keep myself accountable. The responsibility of holding myself to this promise was hard, but it was what I would do. However, the battle of wills continued within me while the night and the sea had a front-row seat to the turmoil in my mind.

"I'm so pathetic." I sighed, swirling the liquid around in circles as if I could erase my shortcomings by doing so.

Absentmindedly, I tucked a loose strand of my hair behind my ear as I took another sip from my glass. Memories flooded my mind, mostly bad, but some good. I thought of Iris and how much I missed her and hoped she was okay.

The guilt I had for leaving her twisted inside of me. I could have done more to find her, I knew it, but the fear of having to deal with anything related to the Chevaliers had turned me into a coward. I wasn't exactly sure what more I could have done outside of going to the police, but I knew that wouldn't have led to anything because of the Chevaliers' influence all over the state and the country. Hell, their power might have extended all over the world, for all I knew.

"Fuck," I mumbled to myself as another sigh left my lips. All I could do was hope Iris was safe and she was okay, especially with me no longer on the lookout for her.

But she wasn't the only person I was thinking about.

I missed Easton. It felt wonderful to admit that to myself.

I wanted to feel his warmth and to hear his voice. His presence was a comfort that I longed for and hated that I couldn't have. Despite the tangled web we were intertwined in, there was a part of me that needed him, and I couldn't deny the imprint he had made on my life.

I breathed in the fresh evening air and looked out over the stunning view once more before taking one last sip of my wine and turning away from the sunset. Taking a deep breath, I turned around and entered my room to prepare for the rest of my night.

I changed into a long black dress, noting that I wouldn't have to go outside in order to reach this restaurant. Plus, due to the weather not being too cold, a dress this time of year was fine.

I checked the time on my new phone and realized that I had a text message.

Tristan: Did you make it there okay?

Tristan was the only one who had this number, but I was still taken aback by him messaging me at all.

Me: Yes, I'm fine. But I'm assuming you knew that already since you and Gabrielle arranged for me to fly here on your plane.

I stuffed the phone into my purse without a second thought. I made sure to check that I had all the essentials, including my wallet, ID, passport, and room key card in my purse before leaving my room.

I couldn't help but look around as I walked through the historic hotel, making my way down to the front desk. I should have done a better job of memorizing where things were when the front desk clerk pointed things out, but there was nothing I could do about that now.

Stepping into the restaurant, I was momentarily taken aback by the sheer elegance of the setting. There were tables draped in crisp white linens, evenly spaced throughout the dining room, each one adorned with silverware that twinkled under the soft illumination of the candles and warm lights.

I sat down at a table that was set for two and immediately felt self-conscious. I'd never dined alone at a restaurant before. It was always with family, friends, or associates of my parents due to my father's position. I was entirely on my own here.

As I read through the menu, a warmth filled me. I found a sense of empowerment in being here alone. I had plenty of funds to cover anything on this menu, and I was free to enjoy my own company. I decided on their pasta sampler accompanied by a glass of water, keeping my promise to myself that I wouldn't have another drink tonight.

When the waiter served my meal, I took a moment to appreciate the way the food was presented to me before I dug into the delicious meal. I closed my eyes as I chewed, taking a moment to enjoy the happiness that was occurring in my mouth.

I wiped my lips and took a sip of my water. Once I placed it back down, I couldn't help but smile. Eating alone didn't mean that I was lonely. In fact, it was liberating in a way. All of this showed I'd escaped from a toxic environment and retained my ability to find joy within myself.

The thought forced my smile to grow. I knew I would probably look ridiculous, but I raised my glass and toasted my newfound independence and the adventures that awaited me here.

This evening and this trip and the excursions that I'd asked Gabrielle, Tristan's assistant, to help me book would be things I would remember for the rest of my life.

I people-watched as I ate my dinner, choosing to embrace my surroundings instead of looking at my phone. I groaned as I ate the last bit of food I could manage and washed it down with a long drink of my water. As I was wiping my lips with the cloth napkin, my gaze drifted to the entrance of the restaurant. For a moment, I froze at the scene playing out before me.

I watched as a tall man stood near the entrance, and I recognized the silhouette immediately. He had the same broad shoulders and the same confident stride as the man that I had left behind. The sight of him sent my heart slamming in my chest, and I was grateful that I hadn't been holding my glass of water.

Had Easton followed me here?

But when the guy turned around, I realized that my thoughts were wrong. Though he looked like Easton from behind, their faces were nothing alike. The realization left me with a mixture of disappointment and relief, and a part of me wished that he was here.

I shook my head as I tried to shake the results of my overactive imagination. There was no way that the wine I'd had earlier was still affecting me, right? My waiter decided that now was the perfect time to bring my bill, and I charged it to my room. As I made a move to leave, the hairs on the back of my neck stood up. My first thought was fear and who could blame me due to what I was going through?

When I looked around for what might have caused it, I couldn't pinpoint anything unusual.

4

BIANCA

I wiped my hand across my face just before I lifted my hands to stretch. I slept in, but I'd woken up naturally, so I figured it was as good a time as any to get up. It took a moment for me to motivate myself to leave the cozy bed, but I managed. I needed to prepare myself for the day ahead. After all, I had plans for today that I wanted to do, and I refused to allow my temporary laziness to stop me from doing so.

Before I fell asleep last night, I decided that today would be dedicated to exploring Villa Rufolo and Villa Cimbrone. Although both were known for their beautiful gardens and it was wintertime here, I knew that both would still be stunning during this time of year.

Letting out a deep breath and rolling forward, I stood up and stretched again. I ran my fingers through my hair before I threw it into a ponytail to take a relaxing shower. I enjoyed every moment of it as the scent of my lavender and vanilla body wash filled the air. The water that I allowed to pelt my skin did its job and removed the remnants of sleep that I was trying to shake. It also helped loosen my muscles, which I was sure would be aching by the time I arrived back at my hotel once the day was done.

After I finished, I stepped out of the shower and grabbed a fluffy bath towel to wrap around myself. When I was done with my face routine, I made sure not to miss any spots as I applied lotion to every inch of my skin.

Once I finished that task, I made sure to dress in a couple of layers, including a T-shirt and a sweater, a pair of jeans, and sneakers. I knew I would be doing quite a bit of walking today and wanted to be prepared. I packed my purse with everything I thought I might need, including a water bottle and a guidebook that I'd picked up on my way back upstairs from the restaurant the night before, and left my room.

After a quick breakfast at the hotel, I found myself walking to Villa Rufolo, the first stop on my journey. Thankfully, it was pretty close to my hotel, but that didn't stop the slight chill I had while walking to my destination.

As I walked toward it, I could already see glimpses of the landmark standing proudly against the sky. The closer I got, the more my anticipation and expectations grew. I couldn't help but stare as I strolled through the entrance because the charm and beauty of Villa Rufolo caught my attention immediately. I walked through the historic structure, marveling at everything I could see and just how serene everything seemed to be.

As I meandered around the gardens, I noticed that there were small pops of color from the few flowers that were still around in December. To top it off, I had a stunning view of the Mediterranean Sea. I made sure to take photos to memorialize my experience and even asked another tourist if they minded using my phone to take a photo of me.

A quick check of the time told me that it was time to head toward Villa Cimbrone. Thankfully, it was a walkable distance as well, and in about ten minutes, I was standing at the entrance.

Villa Cimbrone was just as beautiful as Villa Rufolo. As I made my way through the gardens, I couldn't help but be thankful that I was here. Sure, the circumstances that allowed me to come here were unpleasant, but being here felt life changing in more ways than one.

And that was before I reached the Terrace of Infinity.

The Roman-like statues, which stood along the fence, provided a gateway to a view that was absolutely breathtaking. Then something hit me. The endless stretch of blue water that met the sky at the horizon was probably why it had gotten its name.

Once I'd taken enough photos to last a lifetime, I found myself walking to the exit with a renewed sense of purpose. The sun had begun to set, streaking the sky in orange and pink as I left Villa Cimbrone.

The beauty of the moment was bittersweet in a way. The scenery was mesmerizing, yet there was something missing. Deep down, it felt as if the sight was too beautiful to be enjoyed alone. It was then that I realized, once again, I wished I had someone here with me. But there was nothing I could do about that now, and I needed to own that this trip was a path to me healing from the turmoil I'd endured.

As I walked toward my hotel, the smell of food hit me. It was then that my stomach growled, reminding me that it had been a while since I'd eaten anything. As I walked by a small café, I decided this would be the perfect opportunity to stop and have something to eat.

I was seated immediately, and I had time to enjoy a glass of water while I waited on my dish. I looked into my purse and fought the urge to turn on my old phone and check any messages I might have received.

That thought quickly fled my head when my waiter served me my dinner, and the smells told me that this was going to be another wonderful experience for my tummy. This time, eating alone didn't feel so earth-shattering, and I decided I needed to make this a part of my routine when I returned to the States.

Once I'd finished my meal, I made sure to thank my waiter and the host for their wonderful hospitality and continued my walk back to my hotel. The streetlights were on now, providing the light I needed to walk down the cobbled streets. The soft sounds of the sea in the distance were comforting and I allowed my thoughts to wander.

Once I reached my hotel, I walked up the stairs and found myself in front of my hotel room. It took me a moment to find my key, but once I was safely locked away in my room, I reflected on my journey so far. I was getting comfortable being alone and depending on myself and discovering how nice it was to slow down and enjoy the simple pleasures in life.

Not only that, but I felt happy despite the emotions and uncertainties about the future that swirled inside of me. Today, I experienced a slice of what Italy had to offer. For that, I was extremely grateful.

After a long day of exploring and visiting historic landmarks, I knew I needed to unwind before getting into bed.

First, I turned the television on to a random station for some background noise, and as I was watching the show, I took my hair out of its ponytail and let it fall onto my shoulders. It took a lot of energy to force myself to stop staring at what was playing on the screen long enough for me to walk into the bathroom so that I could wash some of the grime of the day off my skin. When I'd completed that task, I made sure to put on the soft pajamas that I'd bought specifically for this trip.

As I settled under the crisp white sheets, the scent of fresh laundry surrounded me like a warm hug from home. A hug that I missed, but couldn't bear to think about for longer than a few seconds for fear that I might cry.

I closed my eyes and sighed, hoping that sleep would overcome me, when I heard something vibrate on my bedside table. My gaze narrowed in the direction of where I'd heard the sound, and it took me a second to realize it was my new phone that had buzzed. I assumed it was alerting me to a new message or call. I picked it up, expecting it to be from Tristan, but my heart skipped a beat when I realized it wasn't.

Unknown Number: I hope you're enjoying yourself on vacation, B.

My hand flew to my mouth. How did whoever this was know I wasn't in New York? Did they know that I was in Italy? Better yet, how did they get this number?

I refused to let fear fuel my thoughts, but more questions than I could count flew through my mind. As I tried to piece together the puzzle, it still refused to be solved. I thought about answering the message, but being that I was by myself in another country, that probably wasn't the wisest idea.

Instead, I turned that phone off too because, damnit, I needed to rest. I also didn't want whoever this asshole was to ruin the beautiful day I'd had today. I turned over, laid my head down on the pillow, and stared at the television screen until my eyes started to grow heavy. Then I finally drifted off to sleep.

5

EASTON

THE SAME DAY

I stared up at my ceiling as I watched a glow appear out of the corner of my eye. It was coming from my window as the sun was rising. I normally would have been irritated that I'd let the sun seep in because I left the curtains open. Today it didn't make a difference because I'd lain in bed awake for an hour anyway.

I should get up and pack my bag because I was leaving in thirty minutes and I didn't want to be late, but for some reason, I needed to lie there for a few more minutes before I got up. I needed to just be still and think about what I was about to do.

I was going to get Bianca. I was going to get my girl.

I grabbed my phone and checked my text messages in hopes that I might have missed her call or text back. All I found were unanswered text messages and calls from me to Bianca.

That wasn't going to stop me.

I sat up and removed the covers from my body. I threw my

feet over the edge of the bed and ran my fingers through my hair.

It was go time.

I took a quick shower and grabbed the suitcase I was planning to bring with me. I'd started packing the night before because I didn't want to forget anything, a change from my normal packing the morning of. As soon as I laid the suitcase out on my bed, my adrenaline kicked in.

I was tossing another shirt into my bag when my phone buzzed abruptly on the nightstand.

Who the hell was texting me this early in the morning?

When I picked up my phone, I looked back in confusion. What the hell was Nash doing texting me this time of morning?

> Nash: I wanted to talk to you about the night of the party…

For a second, I wasn't sure how to respond. I wanted to be sympathetic to what was going on, but I also needed to catch a flight to see his sister. And I was pretty sure he didn't know where she was.

> Me: It's fine. You had a shit ton to deal with. Why are you texting me this early?

I almost admitted where I was going but remembered that Tristan told me she didn't want her family to know. I wanted to obey her wishes even though I wasn't the one who'd promised to do so. I also couldn't help but wonder if Nash knew that something was up and was using this as a way to get me to admit to it.

Nash: Couldn't sleep.

Not being able to sleep seemed to be a common theme between us. I was about to put my phone back in my pocket when an idea popped into my head. Maybe I could bring some good news to Bianca. But my bringing this up might lead to Nash asking about his sister.

It was something I was willing to risk.

Me: You should probably try to go back to sleep. By the way, did you hear anything about Iris?

Nash: Shit, I wish I had an update for you, but I don't. Still waiting on Chairman Townsend to get back to me.

I remembered that Nash told me sometime later that Parker Townsend was in charge of all of the Chevalier chapters in New York State, including the collegiate chapters. I assumed that made him a busy man, but how hard would it be to answer this simple question?

Me: That sucks, man.

The moment I pressed send, I went back to doing what I needed to accomplish. As my mind flipped through thousands of thoughts that did nothing but feed into the chaos I was feeling, my only focus was on Bianca. Nash's apology, while significant, paled in comparison to getting out of my apartment on time.

I couldn't fight the grin that took over my face as I thought about how I would be in the air in just a few short hours. I couldn't even begin to predict the expression on her face when she saw me for the first time.

I quickly finished packing, double-checking to make sure that I had everything I needed. I grabbed my wallet and passport from the nightstand and slid it into my pocket as I took one final glance around my room.

Was I missing anything?

When I confirmed once more that I wasn't, I grabbed my book bag and my suitcase before making my way to the door. I stepped out into the hallway and locked my apartment door behind me.

I took the elevator down to the lobby.

The man working at the front desk turned and gave me a small head nod. "Going on vacation, Mr. Beaumont?"

I guess it could be called that. "I am."

"Enjoy your trip."

I gave him a small smile. "I will, thank you."

Stepping outside, the cold air slapped my skin. The wind whipped around me as I headed toward the sleek black car idling in front of my apartment. It would be a short, easy ride, so I would be at the airport in a few minutes. The driver got out of the car and opened the door for me, and I was surprised by what I found.

My father was sitting there, reading glasses on his face and his phone in his hand. He looked up a split second later.

"Easton," he said. He removed his reading glasses and tucked them into his coat pocket for safekeeping, his attention now solely on me.

"Dad," I responded, slightly confused by what was going on. "What are you doing here?"

His lips twitched into a half smile, the closest thing to a

full-blown grin I would ever get from him in such early hours. "Can't a father check in on his son?"

"At six in the morning?"

"Doesn't matter the time. Come on, get in."

I did as he said, and soon the car was heading toward the highway. I waited for my father to break the silence between us since he was the one who had intruded on my ride to the airport. Not that I was keeping anything a secret from my parents, and they had been the ones to help me organize the trip with the private flight.

"Easton," he started, the word loud in the quiet car. "I wanted to be here to support you. Your mother did too, but she had a headache this morning and is trying to get some rest."

"Thanks for helping me plan all of this on short notice and for understanding that I might not be around for the holidays this year."

Dad nodded. "I'm sorry it took as long as it did."

In reality, it hadn't been that long. Dad had lent our plane out to one of his friends, so I had to wait to use it until the next day. All that mattered though, was that I was on my way now.

"I'm glad you're doing this," Dad said, cutting through my thoughts.

"You are?"

He looked me in the eyes and said, "I've seen the way you look at her, son. It reminds me of the way I looked at your mother when we started dating. I still look at her like that most times. I've never seen you happier than when you're talking about her."

Despite the seriousness of the moment, a smile tugged at

my lips. He was right. Bianca brought me happiness I hadn't known I was missing until she entered my life. It just occurred to me that my parents hadn't seen me interacting with Bianca much because we were at college, and she had been doing her best to avoid me. That would change when we returned too.

"Thank you, Dad," I said, and I meant it.

"We Beaumonts love passionately," he said. "It can be our greatest strength and our biggest weakness. Protect yourself and your heart, Easton, but don't be afraid to give it either."

I glanced out the window as I saw the small airport I would be flying out of today. I repeated his words in my mind as I processed what he said. "I won't forget, Dad."

With a final nod of approval, he patted my arm as the car pulled to a stop. "Go get her, son."

I smiled at him and opened the car door, too excited to wait for our driver to do so. As I grabbed my bag, my dad stepped out of the car and gave me a hug before giving me another pat on the back. As I walked toward the airport, the short conversation that I had with my father weighed heavily on my mind. With my father's words in my mind and heart, I was more prepared than ever to tell Bianca how I felt.

And it was about damn time.

6

BIANCA

I walked out onto the cobblestone street near my hotel. The sun was shining, and I felt completely relaxed as I took a deep breath of fresh air. I'd been in Italy for three days now, and today, I was going to visit the Museo della Carta. The museum was nestled in an old thirteenth-century paper mill and was dedicated to the history of papermaking in the region.

As I walked toward the museum, I felt a little nervous. I was exploring yet another place that I'd never been to on my own, and I knew there could potentially be danger lurking around every corner. The text message that I'd received from the unknown number haunted me and made me wonder if the person knew where I was. But I tried to shove those thoughts into a dark corner. I knew I needed to do this because I had to take control of my life.

The museum seemed to be rather small, and I strolled up to the ticket office and purchased a ticket. Once I was inside, I noticed there were displays of ancient papermaking techniques all around. I couldn't help but study the machines that

I could see because I was so stunned by how much history was in this one place.

The hour that I spent in the museum passed by quickly as I immersed myself in learning as much as I could. I made sure to pick up a few things from the gift shop before I found myself bundled up in the back of a car, headed back to my hotel.

The drive back didn't take long, and all too quickly, I found myself stepping out of the car and walking toward the hotel's lobby.

I was so caught up in thinking about my experience that I jumped when someone tapped me on the shoulder and said my name.

"Bianca?"

My heart jumped into my throat as my blood froze in my veins. I whirled around automatically. I gasped as my eyes landed on the tall, muscular man standing behind me. But it was his eyes that held me captive. His green eyes sent a jolt through me as my mouth dropped open. I was as familiar with them as much as I recognized my own.

"Easton?" I said. My voice was barely above a whisper. My mouth was dry, making it hard to speak. There was no way this was a mirage, right?

He nodded before pulling me into his arms. Everything about this hug reminded me of the warmth I felt when I sank into the newly cleaned sheets in my hotel room. We stood like that for a moment in the middle of the lobby, and I didn't care how awkward it looked.

"We need to talk."

My mind raced as I tried to process the fact that he was standing in front of me. I couldn't even make my body return the hug because I was in too much shock. Why was he here? How did he know I was here?

I shook my head, trying to clear my mind so that I could focus on one thought at a time. "What are you doing here?"

Easton glanced around the lobby before looking back at me. "We should probably go to your room, and then we can discuss everything."

I found myself nodding my head. "Let's talk." I was proud of myself for managing to say that.

He gently placed a hand on the small of my back and led me toward the stairs so that we could get to my room. The gesture was simple and featherlike, without any possessiveness, yet it made all the butterflies in my stomach come alive. Every subtle brush of his fingers forced the electricity within me that had been dormant to spark.

A thought passed through my mind as we continued to walk. Did he know exactly where I was staying? Or was he following my lead to my room? His movements were calm and collected, his demeanor betraying nothing. It was hard to tell if he was actively guiding me along or just going along with the flow of my stride.

I briefly looked down at his hands and noticed that he wasn't carrying any bags. Questions swirled in my mind. When had he arrived in Italy? Where was he staying? I couldn't wrap my head around the idea that Easton had traveled halfway around the world to find me.

My eyes moved back up to his face. His hair was slightly tousled, and faint shadows were under his eyes. I assumed he might have been a little tired, but he didn't look worse for wear. I hated that about him. It had to be a crime for him to look this good if he'd managed to travel to Italy anytime within the last couple of days.

We were silent as we walked up to my hotel room. It was as if I was on autopilot, and I wasn't sure how to react. We reached my door, and I quickly opened it, holding the door for him to walk in behind me.

His touch lingered on my back as we walked across the threshold. He refused to step away, instead choosing to let his gaze take in the hotel room as if studying the location that I'd chosen as my hideaway.

I turned around to face him and he spoke first.

"I've missed you, Bianca," Easton confessed, his voice steady but barely above a whisper. The words hung in the air; a confession laid bare in the quiet room.

I felt my heart catch in my throat. I'd been wishing to hear him say those words since I'd left New York.

"I..." My voice trailed off because the words stuck in my throat.

He slowly moved his hand to my face, cupping it gently. His thumb brushed against my cheek in a slow, gentle caress. I felt my breath catch as I looked up into his deep-green eyes. I allowed myself to lean into him, something I'd been wanting to do for so long. All the questions and doubts that I had suddenly melted away because of his touch.

All this was overwhelming. I felt the tears well up in my eyes as I stared into his. Finally, I found the courage to say something.

"Easton," I said, barely above a whisper. "I'm so sorry."

"There's no need to be."

He smiled at me and shook his head. Soon I felt myself being gathered into his tight embrace, allowing my body to be flush against his. We stayed like that for what seemed like hours but were probably only moments before he stepped away and gave me a small kiss on the forehead.

But I had something else on my mind. "Before we say anything else, can you tell me if you've heard anything about Iris?"

He looked puzzled for a moment before he spoke. "I haven't heard anything, and I've been trying to find out more information. I'm hoping I'll have some information after the break."

Fuck. That was weeks away.

"Are you sure? You didn't see or hear anything?" I pressed, desperate for anything he could tell me.

"I promise, Bianca. If I knew anything, I would tell you," he said, his voice softening.

It wasn't what I was hoping for, but for now, I had to take him at his word because I didn't have any other choice.

Easton led me to the couch and said, "We have plenty more to talk about as well."

I was thankful for that because my legs felt weak beneath me. As we settled onto the cushions, I could feel the tension between us grow thicker, among other things.

"Easton," I began, taking a moment to suck in a deep breath and gather my composure. "Why are you here?"

His gaze searched mine before he spoke, "I needed to find you, Bianca."

I frowned, pulling my arms tighter around myself. "But why? And how did you know where I was?"

"Why didn't you tell me that you were leaving the country?"

"Because I didn't know what you might do if you knew my

plan. I didn't want to drag you along with me either. Now answer my questions."

He paused as he studied me carefully. "Because there were things I wanted to say to you. Things I should have said a long time ago."

The words hung in the air between us, heavy with an emotion I couldn't quite explain. A range of emotions swirled within me, and I felt as if I was barely hanging on by a thread. I was surprised, confused, and there was a small spark of hope in the pit of my stomach as well.

"What is it?"

His eyes shifted away from me as his leg bounced up and down. I was slightly confused about his reaction because it might have been the first time I'd ever seen him appear to be nervous.

"So, the party that your parents were throwing, which was supposed to turn into your engagement party... What was it? Three days ago, now?"

I nodded in encouragement, even though I wasn't sure of the timing either.

"There was no way I was going to allow you to become engaged to Tristan Whitmore."

I didn't hear that right. I was so shocked by his declaration that it took me a few seconds to find the words to respond.

"But why? What does it have to do with you?" I asked. The spark of hope had begun to bloom, but I needed to hear him say what I thought he was alluding to.

Easton paused before responding. It was as if my question had forced his eyes back to mine and he calmly said, "Because I love you, Bianca."

7

BIANCA

y heart stopped. I blinked hard, certain I'd misheard what he's said. His words echoed in my head as if I couldn't understand what he was saying.

"W—what?" I asked, my voice a mere whisper. I couldn't hear it over the sound of my heart slamming in my chest.

"Because I love you, Bianca," he said once more.

This time, I believed him. His eyes held mine, allowing me to see the truth behind them. Even as those three little words completely knocked my world off its axis. If I'd thought what I'd done before leaving Brentson was enough to cause an explosion, Easton had caused his own by arriving here and saying those words.

My mind raced as a whirlwind of emotions filled me again, or hell, maybe they never stopped. I had imagined, hoped, dreamed of hearing those words from him, more so since he'd thrown out that we should get married to save me from having to marry Tristan. But now that he'd said them, they seemed to hang in the air, and that both excited and terrified me.

Love. The word had thrown me for a complete loop. How could a simple term be so complicated? The word made my heart throb with joy, but it also shattered into a billion pieces.

"But why tell me this now?" My voice trembled slightly.

I was proud of myself for getting that question out because my mind was in a state of chaos. I had so many thoughts that were now forcing me to spiral. How did he know anything about Tristan?

"Because I was going to tell you at the party and probably make a spectacle out of both of us. But you weren't there and something else happened."

He didn't know that I knew exactly what had gone down. Because I'd been the catalyst. I guessed it was time for me to come clean as well.

"Are you referring to the news about my father?"

This time, he raised an eyebrow at me as he stared me down. "How did you know about it?"

I sighed heavily and looked at the floor between our feet. This wasn't how I expected to tell anyone the news, let alone Easton.

"Well, it made national news and... I was the reason why it happened."

A heavy silence fell between us. I could sense the confusion from Easton as he tried to make sense of what I had just said. It was my turn now to explain whether I wanted to or not.

"What happened?" he asked softly, easing my nerves enough for me to tell my story.

"I made a deal with Tristan. In exchange for us not getting

engaged, I needed to provide him with some information about my father because he'd heard some rumors about him. Tristan didn't give me any clues about what the news was or how my father might be involved. I went home and found the evidence and reported it to him. Well, some of the evidence. There was a video that I had no part in finding, and I still wonder if Tristan was sitting on that already and was waiting to see what I would find."

"Wow," he said.

A part of me was happy that he didn't say more. It seemed as if I wasn't the only one who had been left speechless in the last hour.

"You brought down your father and your family's political dynasty."

"I wouldn't call it a dynasty, but sure. I brought him down." I paused and licked my lips, which had suddenly gone dry. "I know of some of the people's lives he ruined on his way to becoming Brentson's mayor. And when he turned on me, I knew I would do anything to prevent his plan from being enacted. I had an opportunity to flip the tables, and I did it. Tristan is also the reason why I'm here right now."

I watched as the tension in his face lifted. He now understood why I did what I did. "He's the reason why I'm here too."

I tilted my head to the side. "He told you where I was?"

Easton nodded. "And called me out for not admitting to myself or you that I loved you."

Why was this day full of surprises? "He did?"

"Yes. And he was right. I should have told you instead of keeping it to myself. I should have said something when you called me out for proposing to you to stop your engagement."

That was a moment I really didn't want to rehash, but I understood why it should be brought up. The proposal had been a disaster, but I couldn't blame him because it had come about as a result of his wanting to help me. However, it wasn't the proposal I wanted from him.

"Do you know what else I should have said?"

I shook my head. "What's that?"

Easton took a deep breath and began. "From the moment we met, I knew there was something special about you. Not only did I know that there was something about you, I also knew there was something about us together that I couldn't quite put my finger on. After the first evening we'd spent together, you were fiery and infuriatingly stubborn, but I enjoyed every second of it," he said, ending it with a faint smile that lifted the corner of his lips, now forming a smirk.

"I felt the same, even when I was pissed at you for how you treated me," I confessed. This wasn't the time to keep my thoughts to myself.

"I'm sorry about that again. It's not an excuse, but I was trying to find a way to make sure that Nash didn't find out about us because I didn't want to betray him on that deal. Apparently, my plans when I'm not thinking straight aren't the best."

His apology softened my stance, but I wasn't about to let him get away with it. "It happens to the best of us."

This time, Easton chuckled, easing the tension between us. I joined in with a small giggle, and it felt good to be laughing with him again. It was soothing and a change from how I felt over the last few days.

When the moment faded, his gaze narrowed, sobering

the mood in the room. "There's one last thing I want to know."

The seriousness in his voice tightened the knot in my chest. "What is that?"

"I can't lie or take back any of the things that I said, including my love for you. How do you feel about me?"

It had just dawned on me that I hadn't said those special words back. I swallowed hard because, even though I knew how he felt, saying the words to him felt as if I was ripping the Band-Aid off and the dam was about to burst.

"Yes," I finally said out loud. The word hung in the air as if everything in the world had stopped and was waiting with bated breath for Easton's reaction.

Before he could say a word, I continued, giving him the exact words that he wanted to hear. "I love you, too."

Easton exhaled slowly, and I watched as his expression softened. It was obvious to see that he was relieved. His hand found my hand, and he laced his fingers through mine. I sighed as his thumb brushed across my knuckles.

His other hand landed on my cheek and brought my face to his.

Our lips met and everything that had happened over the past few days melted away. All I could think about was how much I wanted to stay in this moment forever. His kiss was soft and gentle, and I wondered if he, too, was trying to savor every second of our embrace. He let my hand go so that he could lean into me. As if getting closer to me was a matter of life or death.

I shivered as our kiss turned more intense, his other hand landing on my cheek, anchoring my lips to his.

When he finally pulled back, both of us were left panting

as we tried to catch our breaths and slow our racing hearts. I was convinced that had been the most passionate kiss we'd ever shared, and I assumed it was due to our confessions.

"You know," Easton paused for a moment and then he said, "I want to do something special for us."

"Like what?"

"You'll just have to wait and see."

But when he didn't make a move to get to any of the planning, I grew suspicious. "You already had this planned, didn't you?"

He shrugged. "That's for me to know and you'll see later."

8

BIANCA

A few hours later, I found myself standing in front of the mirror in my hotel bathroom. I did my best to take my time in doing my hair, but I was still speeding through it as if I was running in a track meet. I was excited and nervous about tonight because I didn't know what Easton had planned.

I blow-dried my hair, enjoying the vanilla scent of my leave-in conditioner as it drifted through the room. When that was over, I ran my fingers through my strands, enjoying the way my hair felt. Once my hair was done, I made sure to pin most of it back from my face so that small wisps of it framed my face. It also made it easier for me to do my makeup without me having to worry about my hair getting in the way.

I wanted my face to be as flawless as possible, but I didn't want my makeup to look caked on, so I worked carefully to not apply too much foundation. Thankfully, the number of times I'd been forced to do my makeup for dinners and fundraisers had helped me become more efficient at applying my makeup the way I like. I let out a deep breath after I made sure that my foundation evened out my complexion without making it look heavy. I added a smoky eye that included blending deep grays and mascara that made my lashes look voluminous. To top things off, I put a deep-red lipstick on my lips, and I couldn't help but be reminded of my favorite red wine when I looked at it.

After looking myself over once more, it was time to figure out what to wear tonight. I had brought a few dresses with me just in case I wanted to dress up while I was here, and I was glad I had.

I looked at my hair once more and decided that pinning my hair up wasn't the vibe that I wanted to go for.

As I took out the hairpins that I used to pin my hair back, there was a knock on my door. I was so startled that I threw my hand over my chest, and I almost checked to see if I'd literally jumped out of my skin. I grabbed my phone to check what time it was. It was too early for Easton to be here, and as far as I knew, no one else should know I was here.

So, who in the hell was that?

Fuck. Could it be my stalker?

I tightened the belt of my robe as my heart leapt into my throat. I made my way to the door and let out a sigh of relief because of what I saw on the other side. I opened the door and found a hotel staffer standing there with a package.

"Miss Henson?" he asked.

"Yes."

"This is for you," he said as he handed me the white, rectangular-shaped box that had some weight to it.

"Thank you," I replied and when he walked away, I closed the door behind him.

While everything appeared to be normal, in the back of my mind, I couldn't help but think that this was the person who had been tracking me for who knew how long, playing some sick trick on me.

I walked over to my bed and placed the box down on it. When I finally opened it, my breath caught in my throat. The first thing I noticed was an envelope on top that was addressed to me. Before I opened it, I pulled out an absolutely gorgeous dark-green dress. I stared at it for a moment, slightly starstruck. The fabric was soft against my fingertips, and I couldn't wait to put it on.

Accompanying the dress was a pair of black heels.

I unsealed the envelope and removed the note from its resting place.

Bianca,

This is for you to wear tonight. While I'm sure you'll wear the hell out of it, I can't wait to see this dropping to the floor later on.

Love,

Easton

Not only did the promise of what tonight would bring send a tremble through me, but rereading the word "love" over and over again made me smile. Tonight was going to be amazing and there was no doubt about that in my mind. There was also the relief that none of this was coming from my stalker.

I could feel the butterflies in my stomach as I changed into the beautiful dress that Easton had sent to me. The soft fabric of the dress draped over my curves, hugging me in all the right places, further proving that the tailoring was executed to perfection. In fact, it fit me so perfectly that it made me wonder if it was actually made for me.

I stepped into my shoes and walked back into the bathroom to check myself over once more. Every strand of hair was in its proper place and my makeup was still flawless. When I grabbed my phone, there was another knock on the door.

The screen on the device lit up, confirming that it was the time that Easton had told me he wanted to meet up. I stuffed my phone in my purse and grabbed my coat before making my way over to the door.

I looked out of the peephole to make sure it was him. With a slow and steady breath meant to calm my nerves, I reached for the door handle. I pulled the door toward me and watched as Easton's gaze swept over my body.

The way his eyes moved, showed me he was taking in every inch of the image in front of him. My cheeks warmed at his appraisal, and I smiled as it seemed he liked what he was seeing. I could tell that he was trying his best not to grin too broadly as well.

He, too, was dressed to impress. His tailored dark suit fit him to a *T*, and he'd forgone wearing a tie tonight.

"You look stunning," he said, barely above a whisper. His eyes hadn't left me since I'd opened the door. It was as if he wasn't completely convinced I was real and thought I might fade into the night sky, never to be seen or heard from again.

Hell, that was what I'd done just before leaving Brentson.

As I made a move to step into the hallway, Easton stopped me. "Wait, there's something else. Take a few steps back and then turn around."

I made sure that he was holding the door before I followed his directions.

"Now put the things in your hands down and hold your hair up."

"But why?"

"Just do it, princess," his voice dropped slightly.

I couldn't control my body's reaction to his command. I looked over my shoulder at him but still found myself moving my hands toward my hair. I couldn't believe I'd gone from hating that term of endearment to being thrilled whenever he used it. Once I'd done as he requested, I watched as he maneuvered himself to place something cool along my neck. I glanced down and found a small gold crown with diamonds on it that was connected to an equally delicate chain. My mouth dropped open in shock as I felt his soft touch on the back of my neck, making sure that the necklace was fastened.

"I'm so confused," I said as I tried to process why he would have bought me such a thing. If I was being honest, my confusion didn't just start with the necklace. It was simply next in a line of surprises since Easton first appeared.

"This necklace is a reflection of my admiration for you," he said as he walked around so that he could face me. "While I call you princess quite often, you're much more than that to me. You reign supreme in just about every avenue of my life. That is a crown fit for a queen."

His words shook me to my core as I tried to fight the overwhelming urge to cry. Ruining my makeup before we left the hotel wasn't on my agenda. Then again, none of this was. "I hate you for trying to make me cry."

"That is never my intention unless they're happy tears. Are you ready to head out?"

I nodded as Easton grabbed my coat and helped me into

it. Once I had the rest of the things I was planning on taking tonight, we walked out of my hotel room and down to the lobby together, this time opting for the elevator because of the shoes I was wearing.

There was a black town car waiting for us outside of the hotel, and once we were safely in the vehicle, the driver took off. And I still had no idea where we were going.

My hands rested in my lap as we made our way along, nervously shifting because I had no idea what to do with them.

Easton reached over and held one of them, rubbing my knuckles with his thumb. "Everything okay?"

I nodded slowly. "Yes, just somewhat nervous about tonight. You could probably put my nerves to rest if you told me what we were doing." I looked over at Easton and found a smirk on his face.

"I could, but I won't. It's going to be a lovely surprise."

"Could you at least tell me how long it will take to get there?"

Easton leaned over and whispered in my ear, "Not long enough for us to have a quickie in the back seat."

I couldn't help but think about the last time Easton and I were in a car together. He'd been driving and I was in the passenger seat on the way back from Brentson's football stadium. It ended with Easton pulling off into a deserted parking lot and showing me how badly he needed me after his game.

We made small talk for several minutes, and suddenly, the car began to slow down. There was no way that we were far from the hotel, not given how long the drive was. When it started to connect where we were, I turned to Easton and his eyes immediately met mine.

"Here we are, princess," he said as the car came to a stop.

My mouth dropped open, and before I could respond, our driver opened the door for me.

There was no way that we were about to do what my brain was telling me was about to happen.

9

BIANCA

"Wait, are we... but is that...?" I said as I stared past our driver and out to the water. There was no way that I was seeing what I thought I was seeing.

We'd driven to a dock, and now my gaze was trained on the luxurious yacht gently swaying on the water. By the time I'd snapped out of my shock, Easton was out of the car as well. He gave a small nod to our driver and held out a hand for me to take.

"You can't be serious. This is too much." I looked at Easton for a hot second before I turned back to the scene in front of me. This couldn't be happening.

"I am," he said as I took his hand. Easton helped me out of the car. "That is for us tonight."

I nodded softly, finally processing, and accepting the date he'd planned for tonight. Easton lightly squeezed my hand, and together we walked toward the yacht. He kept me steady along the uneven walk, which was something I appreciated in the shoes I was wearing because the thought of slipping and falling wasn't appealing.

As Easton led me onto the yacht, a tall man dressed in a white uniform approached us. He had salt-and-pepper hair on his head and a neat beard framing his face, and his eyes were warm and welcoming.

"Good evening, Signorina Henson, Signor Beaumont," he said with a small smile. "I'm Captain Moretti. Welcome aboard the Serenity. I'll be showing you around."

Both Easton and I shook his hand, and together, we set off to explore the yacht.

The yacht had a soft glow about it and was basically a luxury hotel on the water. Its interior was beautifully decorated with a mix of contemporary and classic themes. With its rich wood floors and plush, cream-colored sofas in the spacious lounge area, it reminded me in some ways of my parents' home. All of this was complemented by crystal accents and chrome finishings.

But what I absolutely loved was the way its floor-to-ceiling windows ensured that you could see just about everything, including the beautiful landscape of the Amalfi Coast.

Captain Moretti brought us up to the upper deck and showed us the outdoor bar, a hot tub, and an outside lounge area. We also stopped by the lower deck that contained a couple of bedrooms and bathrooms for guests.

After the tour, Captain Moretti brought us back to the main level and left Easton and me alone to enjoy our evening, reminding us that the crew was at our disposal should we need anything.

Easton led us to the dining room onboard, where we were greeted by a crew member named Marco. I looked around the dining room space that only had one table in it. The table had two place settings on a white cloth, so I assumed that was where we were supposed to be eating.

Soft jazz music played in the background while glowing candlelight flickered off the walls. It was definitely setting a mood that was romantic and calm. It was something I desperately needed.

Easton pulled out my chair for me, and I sat down before he sat down across from me.

Marco handed us menus, took our drink orders, and excused himself for the time being. We both looked through the menu, deciding on what we wanted to eat and drink for dinner before speaking to each other again.

Easton looked up from his menu and asked, "Have you decided what you're going to eat?"

"Well, I've decided what I want for dessert, but I can't quite settle on anything for dinner."

He responded with a smirk before he said, "I'm not even surprised."

This time, I looked up from what I was reading. "Hey. What is that supposed to mean?"

Easton chuckled and ran a hand through his hair and briefly drew my attention to it. "It means I've noticed when we've eaten at parties with one another, you usually choose dessert quickly, but you spend most of your time trying to decide what will be your main meal."

I thought about it for a moment and soon realized that he was right. I did tend to do that, but I hadn't realized it before, much less that anyone had noticed. Apparently, being surprised was the mood of the night.

When Marco returned, he brought two glasses of white

wine and some bread. We placed our orders: seafood pasta for me and grilled sea bass for Easton.

Easton cleared his throat as he raised his glass. "To the perfect evening," he said, his eyes meeting mine.

I clinked my glass against his and took a sip. The delicate taste of the wine greeted my lips, and my eyes fluttered closed. I took my time enjoying the sensations that were hitting every single one of my taste buds. I could have sworn that I tasted hints of vanilla and cherry. It was then that everything else faded into the background. It was just Easton and me, under the starlit sky, drifting along in the middle of the ocean. The rest of the world could wait. For now, this was our special place and no one else existed.

As we waited for our meal, we sipped on our wine and engaged in light conversation. Tonight wasn't about the shadows that crept around every corner of our lives, determined to pounce whenever there was an opportunity. This was about Easton and me reconnecting and being with one another.

The night was the epitome of romance, and I could barely feel that we were moving as our captain did a masterful job of guiding the vessel. If I didn't know any better, I could have sworn we were floating on air rather than across water. This moment in time felt absolutely surreal and I wondered if anything would be able to top it.

While I was staring out at the pretty lights that we could see reflecting off the water, our meal arrived. The food looked as good as it smelled. The seafood pasta was delicious. Easton seemed just as happy with his sea bass. We ate slowly, savoring every bite as we enjoyed each other's company.

As we finished our dinner, Easton looked at me and said, "How do you feel about trying out the Jacuzzi?"

I couldn't help but smile. Without a moment of hesitation, I nodded, agreeing to go with him. I wiped my lips before we stood up, and Easton guided me out of the dining room and down to the lower deck into one of the yacht's bedrooms. There, I found another white rectangular box that I assumed contained our bathing suits.

I handed him the swim trunks before I concentrated on the black bikini he'd bought for me. It was a stereotypical bikini, but based on Easton's reaction, you would think that I was completely naked. I couldn't resist putting on a small show as I undressed because I could feel Easton's eyes on me. He dragged his eyes up and down my body, leaving me a heated mess in his wake. Which was interesting given that we hadn't even made it to the Jacuzzi yet. Would we even make it outside of this room?

"You really thought of everything, huh?" I asked, trying to defuse some of the tension in the room. Over my swimsuit, I put on the cover-up that he'd also bought for me.

"I did. I wanted to make this as wonderful of an experience for you as possible. You know..." his voice trailed off and I waited for him to continue what he was saying. "I was going to wait to tell you how much I loved you until tonight in hopes that you would even want to go on this evening's adventure. But I couldn't wait."

My lip trembled at the gravity of his words. "It didn't matter where you said the words. All that matters is that you did and that I feel the same."

Easton closed the distance between us, pressing his body against mine. My senses were filled with him, and I pressed my hand to his chest, allowing the beating of his heart to soothe me and excite me at the same time. I was drawn to his lips, wondering when he would take the plunge and kiss me.

He wasn't in a hurry, and I could sense that he was trying to savor each touch. I couldn't decide if this was the tempo that I wanted him to take. His hands roamed up and down my back as he leaned toward me. My gaze rose to meet his and I saw the heat in his that I was sure matched my own. My eyes fluttered shut as he laid a soft kiss on my lips, sending huge waves of desire crashing through me.

Our kiss lasted for what felt like an eternity and then some and I didn't want it to end.

When I pulled away, Easton rested his forehead against mine. He gave me a small grin before he said, "We should probably head upstairs."

"I agree."

With a small kiss on my forehead, Easton put space between us and grabbed the things we were planning on taking with us to the Jacuzzi. He then held out his hand. I placed mine within his and he led me out of the room, up the stairs, to the upper deck where the Jacuzzi was.

He placed our towels and other items that we might need within arm's reach on a set of lounge chairs as I shivered involuntarily. It was chilly up here, but I hoped with us soon hopping into the Jacuzzi that I would be all warmed up.

I looked out onto the water beyond the yacht, smiling at the gorgeous view from where we were. Then I looked up overhead and noticed how the stars were twinkling above us. We were blessed to have such a clear night that made it easy to see the sky.

"Ready to get into the water?" Easton asked as he walked over to the Jacuzzi before turning back to me.

I had goosebumps on my arms from standing in the open air on deck, so his suggestion made sense. I quickly nodded and pulled the swimsuit cover off my body. Once again, Easton's heated gaze was on me as I hurriedly put my hair into a high bun in hopes of keeping it from getting too wet. Easton stepped into the water first before holding out a hand to help me get in. I sighed as I felt the warmth from the water sinking into my skin. I didn't have to worry about the chill in the air anymore.

Easton sat down across from me after he sank down enough that only his shoulders, upper back, and head were visible above water level.

"Come over and sit on my lap," he said before I could find another place to sit down. The desire in his eyes sent a shiver down my spine, and I couldn't wait to see what else he had up his sleeve.

10

EASTON

The steaming water lapped at my chest as I watched Bianca decide what she wanted to do. While I waited, I basked in the glory of this Jacuzzi, working its magic on my tense muscles.

She moved toward me before settling herself between my legs with a sigh that sounded as if the weight of the world had been lifted off her shoulders. That's one of the things that I wanted for her, and I was more than happy to provide it. I wrapped my arms around her waist and pulled her back against my chest.

She turned her head to look at me and our lips met. Whereas the kiss we shared a few minutes ago was soft and gentle, this one was slow and deep. My need for her continued to build within me as her tongue danced with mine. Although it had only been several days since we'd last fucked, it felt as if it had been months.

I ran my hands up her rib cage, teasing the underside of her breasts because her bikini top gave me easy access to her chest. She moaned softly, the sound vibrating against my mouth. Her hands landed on my thighs, and her nails dug into my skin, stoking the heat inside of me.

Breaking the kiss, I nipped at her earlobe, sending a tremble through her. "How bad do you want this?"

A breathy laugh from her followed. "What do you think?"

"I think we have some lost time to make up for."

She turned in my arms and said, "Then what are you waiting for?"

She'd just thrown down the gauntlet. A challenge that I had no problem accepting.

I slid my hands into her hair and slammed my mouth into hers. She melted against me as her lips parted eagerly for my tongue. My blood was on fire, and I could swear that I felt it pounding through my veins. I couldn't get enough of her taste and the feel of her body pressed to mine.

Her hands roamed over my chest and down my abs, creating an imaginary design that neither one of us could see. I sighed into her mouth, enjoying her soft caress.

"But what about the crew members?" she asked softly.

"They know not to come up here while we're here," I said. My hands had pulled her hair free from the bun she'd placed it in before getting in the Jacuzzi, and I slid it to the side, exposing her neck to me. I trailed my lips down her throat, enjoying the taste of her skin. She arched into me with a soft gasp as her hand made its way to my shoulder to steady herself.

"Easton, please."

"Please what?"

"I want you."

The ache inside me intensified at her plea. I would do anything to make her happy. I gripped her hips and lifted her, setting her on my lap. Her legs wrapped around my waist as she ground down against my dick. A groan ripped from my throat.

"Be careful, princess." I nuzzled her jaw. "We've got all night."

"And I hope we both intend to make the most of it." Her hand slipped between our bodies and her fingers grabbed my cock through my swim trunks. I jerked against her and glared.

"I did warn you." But I was smiling as I captured her mouth again.

I deepened the kiss, tilting her head back to gain better access. Her soft moans drove me and made me want to say fuck taking it slow and take her right now.

My hands traced the line of her collarbone, then slid lower to cup her breasts. I undid her bikini top and tossed it to the side. I rolled one of her nipples between my fingers, then the other, teasing them both and causing her to squirm.

"Easton, please," she sounded desperate, and I couldn't deny that I enjoyed it.

I pushed her back slightly and stuck her nipple in my mouth. She gasped, and her hands flew to the back of my head. I suckled and licked, alternating between the two. The cries that were coming from her lips only fueled my momentum.

I trailed my fingers down her stomach, lightly tickling her skin as I traveled south. She trembled beneath me as I paused at the edge of her bikini bottoms before slipping beneath it. I took my time skimming them over her pussy before making my way to her clit.

I watched as her head fell back as my fingers moved in

circles against her clit, slowly pushing her closer to the edge. I wondered for a moment if the vibration and water from the Jacuzzi were providing another level of pleasure for her. She bucked against me, and her head flew back as a result.

"That's right, princess. Come."

I increased the pressure and moved in a figure-eight motion that caused her breathing to become shallow pants.

Her muscles tensed around my hand before she finally let go.

She slowly opened her eyes and looked at me. She looked slightly dazed. I offered her a big grin before I reached down to remove her bikini bottoms.

"There. That's better," I said.

"You know what would be better? You taking off your trunks and me slamming down on your cock."

"Is that right?"

"Yes," she responded. "That's what I want."

There was no way I was denying her. I smirked and removed my trunks. Then, without breaking our connection, she kneeled down on my lap and slowly lowered herself onto me.

The sensation of me being inside her sent bolts of pleasure throughout my body. We both gasped as we adjusted to the feeling. I put my hands on her waist, and we moved together in perfect harmony.

My heart raced as I pounded into her, and her moans grew louder with every move we made. I pushed deeper into her as one of my hands made its way to her clit, adding extra sensation for her.

When her breathing grew short once more, I knew she was close again.

"Easton," she screamed out as her orgasm hit her. Watching her in the throes of passion had me following shortly after, filling her with my release. I held on to her until our bodies stopped shaking from the intensity of pleasure we just experienced together.

We stayed there for some time, silently holding each other in the Jacuzzi.

Eventually, we managed to get out, wrapping towels around ourselves. I pulled her against my chest as we both looked up at the star-filled sky, our breathing slowly returning to normal.

"That was incredible," she said in awe.

"Yes," I replied. "It most certainly was."

"Thank you."

Her heartfelt thanks shook me, but I managed to control my emotions.

We grabbed our things and made our way back to the bedroom downstairs.

Once there, Bianca walked toward the door, and I raised an eyebrow at her. "What are you doing?"

"Going to take a shower before we head back to the hotel."

"We're staying here for the night."

She did a double take. "Wait, what?"

"I never said the surprises were over. But a shower is a great idea."

"But we don't have pajamas."

"Who said we needed any?"

Bianca chuckled. "You have a good point."

I shrugged. "I did buy some pajamas and robes for us as well."

She walked over to me and gave me a kiss on the lips. "You really did think of everything."

With a slight sway of her hips, Bianca left the bedroom and moved into the bathroom. She dropped the towel so that I could see her bare ass just before she closed the door almost all the way, leaving it only open a crack.

There was no way I wasn't joining her in the shower.

I followed her into the bathroom, and she already had the shower running. We shared a smile and we both stepped underneath the hot water spray.

I watched as she was drenched once more before I made my move. I stuck my finger under her chin and kissed her.

We were supposed to be cleaning off to get ready for bed, but I needed to have my lips on her.

Bianca took a step back and said, "The point of this is to get clean, not dirty."

I smirked back at her. "But I know for a fact that you love getting dirty. In fact, this might be the perfect opportunity for me to fuck you—"

"No," she said as she playfully wagged her finger. "We are going to get clean and then go to bed."

I shrugged my shoulders and went to grab a washcloth and the body wash that I had asked to be stocked. She could think that I wasn't fucking her again tonight, but I had no doubt that we would spend most of the night giving each other multiple orgasms.

I took my time washing her body and she did the same to me. The kisses and caressing continued until Bianca made sure that we both had rinsed our bodies and turned the shower water off.

Afterward, we dried ourselves off with fluffy white towels,

then walked back into the bedroom, where we slipped into the new pajamas.

Bianca walked over to her bag as I moved to the other side of the bed. As I was pulling the covers back, I heard something hard hit the floor, forcing my attention to land back on her. The sight that met me caused me to freeze.

I watched as she swallowed hard before tears began to flow from her eyes. Something in Bianca had shattered, and that realization hit me harder than any physical blow could have.

11

BIANCA

The sudden rush of tears shocked me, and it only fed into the tsunami of emotions that slammed through me. There was nothing I could do to stop the salty teardrops from flowing. The dam had broken, and I couldn't do anything to prevent it.

Easton's mouth dropped open and his eyes filled with concern. Before I could make another sound, he rushed to my side and pulled me into his arms. Being in his arms once more offered a small reprieve from the weight that was bearing down on me. The warmth from his body helped calm me down, but I couldn't stop crying immediately. I was mortified about crying in front of him, but I couldn't control it.

I tried to speak, but nothing came out. Any hope of making a sound that was anything but sobbing, was buried in my throat. Instead, I chose to bury my face into his shoulder and cried. Thoughts of staining his shirt due to my crying flew from my mind and he didn't seem to care either.

After a few moments that seemed to stretch on for longer

than anticipated, I felt Easton adjust his body and then I heard him speak.

"Bianca." His voice was gentle. "Please look at me."

I shook my head, my cheeks burning as the heat crept up my neck. "I'm so sorry, but—" My words died on my lips and my incomplete sentence hung in the air.

"You have nothing to apologize for." He tucked a strand of hair behind my ear, his fingertips grazing my cheek, a gentle reminder that he was here for me. I couldn't help but lean into his touch. "I'm here for you, remember? Through every-thing. Now, tell me what happened."

With a heavy sigh, I managed to build enough courage to meet his gaze. His eyes were slightly soft, filled with under-standing, but there was an intensity, a hidden fury there that I was pretty sure wasn't directed at me. However, the look in his eyes did nothing but add to the calmness that was slowly taking over my body and my emotions. The ache in my chest eased a smidge as it hit me. I realized that, in this instance, he was an anchor for me during this emotional turmoil I was experiencing. Which seemed fitting given where we were currently.

"I know," I said before I let out a shaky breath. I felt defeated even though there was no reason for me to feel this way. However, there was now no use in hiding any of this from him. I could easily read the concern on his face, and it was time I put him out of his misery. "I got another text message from my stalker on the phone they shouldn't have the phone number for."

The words carried a lot of weight and admitting it out loud felt like the first step. The tension that floated between us seemed to further darken the cozy vibe we'd had going only minutes before.

Easton slightly tightened the grip he had on my hand. Then he bent down to pick up the phone. The device's screen lit up and I watched his eyes scan the message, taking in every word in the text. I knew what he was reading by heart because I'd already committed the text message to memory.

> Unknown Number: Be careful on the Amalfi Coast, B. Then again, maybe the best place to be is on the ocean.

I watched Easton's face as he read what was on the screen to see if I could get any indication about how he might react. Anger flashed on Easton's face as he stared at the message. His face hardened, and I noticed his jaw clenched and unclenched, but still, he didn't say a word. As his eyes darkened, I could sense his fury growing, but he continued to look at the screen in silence.

He pulled me closer to him, tucking me into his side before he spoke, "How long has this been going on?"

I didn't respond because it felt as if any words I could have said were stuck in my throat. Easton's gaze never wavered from me and the intensity in them only seemed to grow as the seconds ticked by. I should tell him everything that I knew about this person who had chosen to break the boundaries that I'd built. But for some reason, I couldn't say the words that had been on the tip of my tongue for ages.

"I can't help you if I don't know what is going on." Easton's tone was firm, showcasing his determination to get to the bottom of this.

"It's been going on for a while," I finally said as I shifted my gaze. I couldn't bear to look him in the eyes anymore because I was afraid of his reaction. My voice was so soft I barely recognized it. "I think it started when you sent me those apology flowers earlier in the semester."

"You kept this to yourself for that long?" I could hear the disbelief in his voice, and it was another reason why I couldn't look at him.

I shrugged as two fingers on either side of my jaw turned my face so I was looking at him. I wasn't willing to start a fight about when I should have or shouldn't have said something about a situation I was dealing with. "I didn't want to worry anyone, especially with my father's career. I didn't want to make a big deal out of it, so I mostly ignored it. It hasn't extended past text messages as far as I know and—"

"Listen, no one fucking stalks you and gets away with it. Whoever is doing it will have to answer to me. It's my job to protect you," he said, and I knew, without a doubt, he was serious. Dead serious.

I was caught off guard by his words. "What do you mean about 'protecting me?' Are you talking about hiring security guards for me or something?"

His hand left my jaw and moved to grab my hand. I could have sworn that his touch burned me, but all I could feel were the butterflies that were dancing in my stomach.

"That wouldn't be a bad idea."

My hand shot up, signaling to Easton that I wanted him to stop. "Isn't that a bit extreme? I told you this person hasn't done anything outside of text messages."

"That you know of," he said, throwing my own words back in my face with a small grin. "But seriously this person clearly knows your every move."

I swallowed hard. "That's a good point."

His pointed stare seared a hole through my heart and straight into my soul as he said, "I don't want you to be alone too often, especially with this person on the loose. Who knows what sort of desperate situation they might be in that would then lead to them taking their efforts up a notch."

A lump rose in my throat, making it feel as if it was almost impossible for me to swallow. Easton's words slammed into me like a freight train. I understood what he was saying and didn't disagree. It wouldn't hurt to be more careful until this was wrapped up.

"You might be right," I said, though it kind of felt as if I was admitting defeat or that I couldn't handle this alone. That was something I needed to deal with. "After all, this person had no problem hunting down my new number, which was attached to an entirely different phone, and finding out I was traveling to Italy. Hell, whoever it is, knows I'm on this yacht right now."

Easton turned to look back at the phone screen and said, "It's late. We should probably get some sleep. Tomorrow morning, we can make some plans about what should happen next."

I nodded, agreeing with his assessment. Whether I would fall asleep easily was an entirely different question, but at least trying to do so made sense. That way, I could also table any discussion of this for the time being.

I climbed into bed and moved over so Easton had plenty of room to join me. He waited until I was settled before turning the lights off and crawling into bed too. He wrapped his arms around me, and a soft, sad smile covered my lips. Being in his arms made me feel safe and protected, providing a sense of serenity that I hadn't felt in such a long time. How nice that was, seeing as we were on a yacht of the same name.

I flipped around so that my head landed on his firm chest, where I could hear the steady beating of his heart. It was as if it was a sweet lullaby that helped me shift gears so that I was only thinking about turning my brain off. Nothing else mattered now, and I would embrace that feeling wholeheartedly, at least for the time being.

We soon fell asleep to the sound of waves crashing outside our window. I was temporarily at peace.

12

EASTON

The cool ocean breeze slid across my face as I paced along the wooden deck of the yacht I'd rented for Bianca and me. It was our temporary sanctuary that was supposed to be our saving grace after everything in the world we'd lived in had gone to hell, especially for Bianca. The sight of the picturesque blue sea was jaw-droppingly beautiful and went out as far as the eye could see. This should have been a peaceful morning, but it was anything but due to some asshole who'd managed to figure out that Bianca was in Italy.

We were near the island of Capri, according to what one of the crew members told me just moments before I stepped out there. But despite the enchanting view, there was something weighing heavy on my mind.

My eyes were drawn to my cell phone. I'd managed to grab it out of my pants without waking Bianca. My intention was to take it in case I wanted to make the call I'd been debating with myself about since last night. I glanced at my phone's screen and noticed I did have cell service. I'd thought we might have it since we were close to the shore, but sometimes you never knew. This would hopefully make it easier for my call to connect. Well, if I was going to make the call at all.

I found a lounge chair, sat down, and quickly found Nash's number. There was some guilt deep within my heart as my finger hovered over the button that would start it all. Bianca should be the one to tell him this because it was her story to tell.

But we'd already lost precious time since she'd kept this to herself. And I wouldn't feel guilty about doing all that I could do to keep her safe. Having access to Nash's resources would be nothing but an asset. If we were working on this alone, it would take us much longer to get results outside of outright using Bianca as bait for this stalker. Hell, we didn't even know the reason why this person was stalking Bianca, to begin with.

I rubbed a hand down my face in an effort to calm down the million-and-a-half racing thoughts that were flying through it. I pressed the dial button, and the call immediately went to voice mail. I waited a beat before calling the number again.

This time the phone rang several times, and I tapped my index finger on the armrest as I waited for Nash to answer.

"Hello?" His voice was filled with sleep.

I internally winced as I cursed to myself. How could I have forgotten about the time zone difference? "I'm sorry, I forgot that it was like one a.m. there."

While I did regret calling him this early, I didn't regret calling him completely. It was important for him to be in the loop on this.

"It's fine," he mumbled. His tone told me that "fine" was the last thing he felt in regard to being woken up at this time. He yawned for good measure, and I couldn't help but wonder if he did it loudly for my benefit. "I would be more pissed if you'd woken up Raven. Give me a second."

I heard some rustling in the background, and I assumed it was Nash leaving his bedroom and heading somewhere else where he would have the opportunity to talk freely.

"Why are you calling me this late, dude?" His voice was now mostly clear of the grogginess it had been filled with, but it had been replaced with something else. Now it seemed as if he was curious about why I'd called, but there was a smidge of irritation there as well. I couldn't blame him for that.

When he didn't ask me what I meant about me alluding to the time zone difference, I took it as a blessing. "There's something I need to tell you, but you have to promise to keep it mostly between the two of us outside of what I want you to potentially investigate."

"How serious is this?" I could hear the gears in his head turning all the way from here.

"Very serious," I said, and I could swear I heard my heart pounding in my chest. "It involves someone that you and I care a lot about."

There was a brief pause on the other end before Nash responded, "You have my word. What's going on?"

I took a deep breath and knew I needed to just say what I needed to say and get it out there because I was over the debate I'd been having with myself. "Bianca has a stalker."

The line went quiet except for Nash's breathing. It was the only thing that told me he was still on the line. "What has been going on? Is that why we haven't been able to reach her? Is she okay?"

I hated that I had to spring this on him about his sister, but it was the only choice I had.

"She's fine and has just been lying low with me due to all the news. As far as we know, it's just been text messages, but they've been getting more and more specific." I was toeing a fine line about telling him about where we were. Hell, would he say something about Bianca and me being somewhere alone together?

There was a brief pause before Nash spoke. "Funny. Something similar happened to both Raven and me too."

I was surprised by both the revelation and his lack of questioning my intentions with his sister. Maybe he'd fully moved on from that, but what I needed to do was focus on Bianca's safety.

It was then a new possibility appeared in my head. I wasn't sure if this theory would be welcomed or not, but I needed to get it out there to see what Nash thought. "I wonder if all three of these instances could be related?"

"They could be...hmmm. We should compare notes on them."

Fuck.

I didn't want to end Bianca's vacation early, but it did make sense that we should talk about this in person. Her safety was the most important thing, and if this would help guarantee it, then so be it. I could also take her on another trip and spoil her there.

I cleared my throat. "Look, she's safe with me for the time being. We'll hang low and then meet up in a few days. Before the holiday rush really kicks off?"

I hoped that was enough to slightly push Nash away from wanting to meet right now. Bianca and I needed to get back to the United States, preferably without detection from Nash or anyone else.

"If that's what she wants. Where is she anyway?"

"Sleeping." At least that wasn't a lie. While the rest of our world was in motion, Bianca was getting the rest she deserved, unaware of what I was currently doing.

"Okay. I'll talk to her later then." He stopped speaking for a moment and as I was about to say something else, he started speaking again. "You know what? This is partially my fault."

I did a double take. "Wait, what? How?"

Nash sighed and I could hear the regret in it. "I thought Tomas was the one behind the text messages that were being sent to Raven and me. It ended when we took him down, but obviously, he wasn't the culprit."

There was very little I knew about Tomas due to him being the chairman of the Chevaliers before I became a member. But Nash was right. If Tomas currently didn't have the ability to do this, then who the hell was sending these text messages?

"Would it make sense to talk to him? Could it be someone connected to the Chevaliers?"

"I don't know if we could talk to him or if he would want to talk to us at all. And I'm not sure it's someone related to the Chevaliers, but I'll find out if it is..."

Nash didn't need to elaborate on what he would do because I already knew. And I would be joining him in that crusade.

"Could this be connected to Iris's disappearance?" The question just appeared from the corner of my mind.

Nash yawned loudly in my ear. "I'm not sure, but I'm hard-pressed to believe that Soren Grant would have taken Iris while watching Bianca. That's a lot of work... unless he's working with someone else."

"And we still don't know if she's okay or not."

"True, and I am still hoping to get more clarification on that soon..." Nash's voice trailed off. "Okay, I'll see what I can do on my end until we meet up."

"Thanks, and I'll let you get back to sleep."

"I'll reach out when I have more information. We'll hunt this asshole, Easton."

"I know."

I ended the call and glanced back at the stairs. Bianca was still asleep, blissfully unaware of the morning's conversation. I took a moment to gather my thoughts and decided that I would end this if it was the last thing I did.

13

BIANCA

I could feel my body starting to wake up, but I didn't want to. Sleep was where I could forget about all the troubles of the world, and I wanted to stay there. I blinked my eyes as I tried to clear the sleep, but it didn't help that I was disoriented. I didn't recognize anything in the room I was in, from the colors to the luxurious sheets I lay on.

Confusion muddled my mind. *Where the hell am I?*

I closed my eyes again. For a moment, I couldn't put it together, but then I heard something that sounded familiar. The steady, almost rhythmic sound of waves.

My eyes snapped open and the confusion that I felt was lifted. The jagged pieces that held the location of where I was finally snapped into place. I remembered that I was in Italy. I was safe in one of the bedrooms on the yacht that Easton had rented for us. I sighed as the realization of it washed over me, causing the tension within me to ease.

I frantically scanned where I was as my eyes darted left and then to my right. Where was Easton? I ran a hand down the side of the bed he'd gone to sleep on, and it had long cooled.

I took a shaky breath as I threw the covers off my body and shivered as I stepped onto the floor. There was a slight breeze in the air, and it raised goosebumps across my skin. I stretched my body and reached for the fluffy white robe that I'd laid across the foot of the bed. It covered the pajamas that I had on, and I walked out of the bedroom, determined to find Easton.

I tiptoed down the hallway, being careful not to make too much noise even though we were the only guests on the yacht.

But I was convinced I was creeping around because all I could think about were the texts on my phone. Whoever it was, they knew where I was.

He was out there. Somewhere. And he was tracking me.

But this person couldn't reach me here. I was safe.

Yet there was a voice in the back of my mind that openly mocked me and said, "Liar."

Nowhere was safe anymore, not even in Italy.

As I stepped out onto the main deck, I shaded my eyes in an attempt to keep the sun from blinding me. A light, salty breeze touched my face, and for a second, I could almost forget what was happening in my life.

Almost.

"Good morning."

I whirled around as my heart leapt into my throat. But it was only Easton, sitting on a lounge chair as a concerned frown crossed his face.

He put his hands up and said, "It's only me out here."

"Sorry," I muttered and looked away from him. "I guess I'm still a little jumpy from the text messages that I was sent."

"I don't blame you." His frown deepened and I hated that my situation put that look on his face.

I looked away, biting my lip. Gazing at the ocean was a much better experience than having to think about this person stalking me.

"Hey." His hand appeared on my shoulder, and I hadn't realized he'd left his seat. "We're going to fix all of this. I promise. And if the person who is stalking you so much as hurts a hair on your head, I'll..."

His voice trailed off, but the vow he'd made was clear. And it was something I needed to hear. I turned to face him and could see the determination in his eyes. My relationship with him had turned from not being sure if I could trust him at all to believing he could find the person stalking me.

"We should head out and explore Capri," he said as he ran his hand through his hair. "It would be nice to take your mind off... everything."

A perfect day with Easton sounded like a dream, something I'd longed for since stepping foot into Italy. No responsibilities, no fears, no looking over my shoulder.

"We can't avoid Brentson forever though," he added. "Eventually we'll have to head home and face all of this."

I hated that he was right. But I didn't want to go back. Having to face my stalker, my parents, and everything else I'd left behind sounded like pure hell. It caused a flood of panic and dread within me, something that refused to be contained.

"Bianca?" Easton turned back to me. "Did you hear what I said?"

I swallowed hard, forcing a small smile. "A day exploring Capri sounds perfect."

It wasn't a lie. I couldn't think about the rest of the things he'd mentioned.

"Good. I want this to be a day both of us will always remember."

"I'm sure it will be."

I COULDN'T HELP but smile at the scenes in front of me. The streets of Capri twisted and turned, awash in color and scent. The colorful homes and storefronts were cheerful, something I'd tried to fully embrace as we walked down the streets of the city. Easton tucked my hand in the crook of his arm as we strolled down the street, pointing out sights we would come across. I found myself completely lost in the charm of this island.

Well, almost.

In the quiet moments between the two of us, the fear crept back in. Questions about how the stalker was able to find out where I was and my new number from a phone that was bought by Tristan's company were never far from my mind.

We stopped at a tiny café for lunch, and I couldn't help but notice the tables scattered around the courtyard that were filled with other patrons. They were busy chatting among themselves, much in the same way Easton and I were. He reached over and held my hand, his gaze showing the tenderness I'd craved.

If only we could stay here forever.

But we couldn't.

That thought alone was enough to sour the ravioli capresi I had for lunch. Still, I forced myself to enjoy every single one of these moments.

We spent the rest of the day exploring Capri, and as the sun began to set, we made our way back to the yacht in silence. Neither of us wanted to leave.

By the time we boarded the vessel, dusk had fallen. The crew was busy preparing for us to sail back to Ravello, but Easton and I stood at the railing, allowing the light breeze to wash over us.

"This is like something out of a dream," I said softly.

"It is." Easton's arm slid around my waist. I wished that I could feel the warmth from his body, but my clothing prevented that. "We'll come back. Once this is all over, I'll take you anywhere you want to go. No more running or hiding or looking over your shoulder."

I leaned into him, clinging to the hope and determination in his voice and the promise that he'd made.

We stayed like that for what seemed an eternity before Easton finally pulled away. But he didn't go far. He laced his fingers with mine and led me to the dining room. The crew, once again, had laid out a romantic dinner for us, complete with candles and rose petals on the table.

The sun slowly disappeared as we ate our meal and drank our wine. We kept the small talk light, I assumed, for fear of it treading into discussing my stalker or my father's career. We talked until late into the evening, and I finally began to get sleepy from exhaustion.

Easton rose from his seat and helped me up from mine so that we could head downstairs and go to bed. Tomorrow was a brand-new day, a day that would draw me out of my hiding place and back home to where I needed to be.

14

BIANCA

I sighed as I surveyed the scene before me. The hotel room, which I'd managed to keep clean throughout my entire stay, was now a chaotic mess. Everything I'd brought with me to Italy, along with the souvenirs I'd bought, were strewn across the room in complete and utter disarray. I was convinced that either I needed to buy another bag or find a way to get creative in order to get all these things into the bags I brought along with me. The former would make things easier, but the latter would provide a challenge I was tempted to accept.

As I started to fold my things, I couldn't help but think of everything that had happened on this unforgettable trip. I ran my fingers over the pajamas that Easton had bought for me as a surprise on the trip along the Amalfi Coast on a private yacht. How much I wished that I could be back there and listening to the calming sound of the ocean waves instead of standing here packing to head home.

I jumped slightly when there was a knock on the door, stopping my thoughts in their tracks. To say I was startled was an understatement. It was as if my heart had stopped beating in anticipation of something bad that was about to happen. Easton said he would be back soon, but I wasn't expecting him now. Unless that much time had flown by?

I looked at the sleek digital clock on the brown bedside table. The numbers on the clock confirmed that it wasn't time for me to meet up with him yet.

"Who is it?" I asked loudly enough that I didn't have to walk closer to the door.

"Lorenzo from the front desk," a male voice answered from the other side. "I have a delivery for you."

I walked to the door and made sure to look out the peephole before opening it. I confirmed that he was in the uniform that was standard at the hotel. I unlocked the door and pulled it open to reveal a guy holding a manila envelope.

"Delivery for you, ma'am," he said as he handed me the envelope. His eyes didn't meet mine, focusing instead on some point over my shoulder. I wondered if that was nervousness or if something else was up.

I shook my head. I needed to calm down on the paranoia.

"Thank you," I replied, taking the envelope. I tipped him and closed the door.

I turned the envelope over in my hands to see if I could find any identification that could tell me where it might be from. There was no return address, no indication of who might have sent it. That set off every alarm in my mind. Should I wait for Easton to come or just open it now?

The knot in my stomach tightened as I debated with myself before finally coming to a decision.

I walked over to the desk in the room, and I could hear

the blood rushing through my ears as I slid my finger under the flap.

"Shit." The curse escaped my lips as I looked at what was inside.

The photos that tumbled out of the envelope looked all too familiar. The ones with me partying hard on campus.

Son of a bitch.

My stalker was the reason my father had these pictures of me.

This couldn't be happening. Not now.

I scrambled to gather the photos, my hands shaking so badly I could barely hold on to them.

Before I could second-guess myself, I grabbed my hotel key and ran out the door of my hotel room, sprinting down the hallway in my bare feet.

I banged on the door that Easton told me was his when we arrived here twenty minutes ago, and he answered on my first knock. "Bianca? What's wrong?"

I hugged him first because that was all I could think to do. There were no words between the two of us as we stood there enjoying each other's embrace. When I realized that the door was still open, I broke the hug and looked around. There was no one there.

I pushed past him into the room. "I just figured out who sent those photos to my father."

"Who?" he asked as I heard the door slam behind us.

I thrust the envelope at him. He took it with a raised eyebrow, but as soon as he saw what was inside, his eyes widened for a split second.

"So, whoever is stalking you is the one who sent these," he said.

Our eyes met as realization and the gravity of this situation slammed into both of us. There was anger in his eyes once more.

"They are flaunting this in our faces, and I'm going to fucking kill whoever it is."

Fear settled into the pit of my stomach as I watched him fume. Was he being serious? I knew I needed to do something to calm the situation down.

"Easton. I know that this wasn't you," I said as I sank down onto the edge of Easton's bed. It was as if my knees were suddenly too weak to support my body. "Not that I even thought it was you anymore."

"After all of this, I assumed you didn't. I also suspected that Diana Caldwell might be responsible, but unless she hired this person to stalk you, I assume it's not her either," Easton said as he kneeled in front of me. "Sending this to you here when barely anyone knows where you are, might be the first mistake they've made because—"

"It narrows the list of people down. Well, unless someone else leaked that I was here."

Easton took a deep breath. "Let's look at the photos and the envelope. Maybe there's some clue in them that could help us identify who sent these."

"I looked at the envelope already and didn't find anything. I didn't study the photos though. In fact, I don't know if I want to look at them again."

"Why don't we go back to your room since I'm done putting my stuff away, and then I'll look them over while you're packing and can help you if you need anything?"

I nodded because it sounded like a great plan.

I watched as Easton grabbed his things, and together, we walked back to my room.

He sat down at the desk while I went back to the bed and continued packing for home. He didn't say a word, and that made me nervous.

"Did you find anything yet?"

"Not yet. I've been trying to analyze everything in the photos, but I haven't found anything concrete."

"Well, I'm just about done packing, but I might need to buy another suitcase for these things," I said, gesturing to the items still out on my bed.

"You can put them in my bag. I have some room. That way, we can head to the airport without any delays," he said as he stood up.

Easton walked over to me and placed a quick kiss on my lips.

I looked into his eyes and said, "Have I told you how much I love having you here? To not have to face any of this alone?"

He just stared at me as I laid my vulnerabilities bare. He pulled me close again, wrapping his arms around me tightly as if he could protect me from all the shit that was being thrown at me. I wasn't sure he understood how much that meant to me.

"I love you too." He leaned down and gave me a more meaningful kiss before he broke away. It was go time.

There was another knock on the door, but this time Easton answered it. Another uniformed hotel staff member walked in with a professional smile on his face.

"Good morning, Signorina Henson, Signor Beaumont,"

he greeted. His eyes caught sight of our luggage. "I am here to collect your bags for checkout."

"Thank you so much," I said as he walked into the room.

He neatly stacked our suitcases on a cart. I did one last run-through of the room to make sure I didn't leave anything behind before joining Easton in the hallway. Together, we walked downstairs and made it to the reception desk.

Checking out of the place that I'd called home for several days had been quick, almost too quick. I appreciated the hotel's desire to get us on our way, but it still felt as if I was being ripped from a place that had been, for the most part, safer for me to be.

Outside of my stalker finding out where I was.

My eyes were darting every which way as Easton escorted me out to the black town car we were going to take back to Naples airport. I put my seat belt on once our bags were in the trunk. He spoke to the driver for a minute before he eased into the seat next to me. As soon as he shut the car door, I grabbed his hand and put it on my lap.

To say I was nervous about what I would find when I returned home was an understatement. But if I had Easton by my side, I knew I had someone to lean on.

And that would get me far.

15

BIANCA

The engines of the private jet roared to life as Easton put his hand on my lower back to guide me up the stairs and into the luxurious cabin. My heart pounded, hands trembling at the thought of flying back to the United States. But here we were.

I sat down and Easton settled into the seat beside me before turning to look at me. He took my clammy hand into his and rubbed small circles over my knuckles. "We're going to make it past this. *You* are going to make it past this."

I wanted to believe him. His words should have been a source of comfort, but they had no effect on me. Nothing was getting past the fear that crowded my mind.

The plane sped down the runway and ascended into the air, sending my stomach lurching. I squeezed my eyes shut as panic settled in. I'd been nervous when I'd left New York, but it was nothing compared to what I was feeling as we started our return trip.

Easton pulled me toward him and stroked my hair. "Breathe with me," he whispered.

When I opened my eyes, we were cruising high above the clouds. It was peaceful up there. Several deep breaths allowed me to rest my head on Easton's shoulder as the tension slowly left my body.

Easton was absolutely right. I could beat this, and having him there with me would be an added bonus. The path ahead might be difficult, but there was a spark of hope that hadn't been there before. The one he had ignited. That I could now rely on.

The ride back to the United States was uneventful. Easton and I ate, chatted, and napped as the hours ticked by. The plane touched down with a gentle bump, jolting me from a light doze. I rubbed the sleep from my eyes and peered out the window at the familiar landscape of Upstate New York.

As we taxied, Easton squeezed my hand and asked, "Are you ready?"

I swallowed hard but nodded. It was time to face whatever awaited me.

We made it through customs and climbed into the back of another black town car, and soon the driver he'd hired was maneuvering the exit procedures of the local airport. This meant, unlike the ride I'd had from Brentson to New York City, which gave me hours to prepare to leave the country, my time to prepare to be back in Brentson would be much shorter. I didn't say a word as I stared out the window at the rolling hills and patches of forest, trying to prepare myself for what could potentially be coming.

When we finally turned onto my street, I couldn't shake the dread that took over. The tension hit me in a suffocating wave as we approached my apartment.

This was it.

I was home.

Once we were standing outside of my apartment door, it took me a second to find my keys. As I unlocked the door, I was hit with a wave of emotion I tried to keep at bay.

As I pushed open the door and took the opportunity to scan my apartment, it was the same as I'd left it, yet it still felt foreign to me.

My throw blanket was still over the arm of my couch. My book bag with the things I took with me to my last day of classes was still resting on one of my barstools. I eyed the bottle of wine that was still on my kitchen counter. My nerves were shot, and it was taking a lot for me to not reach for it, but I felt a sense of achievement at not doing so.

Then it hit me.

It was me that had changed. And that was something I needed to come to terms with, in addition to dealing with my demons.

Easton turned to me and said, "I'm going to look around. Make sure we're alone and no one was here."

"But nothing is disturbed," I protested.

"That doesn't mean someone wasn't, or isn't, here. Humor me by waiting here until I check everything?"

What harm would it do? "Fine. I won't move from this spot."

Easton gave me a small, tired smile and went off to look through my apartment to see if anyone had entered it. My building was pretty secure, but you never knew what could happen.

I twisted my torso slightly to look behind me to see if there were any marks near my front door that would indicate someone had tried to come in, but there were none.

I pulled out my old phone from my purse and turned it on as I was somewhat ready to face what was coming to me. When my phone's alerts started to sound, I immediately turned my phone on silent to save me the headache of having to hear it.

As I was looking through my messages, I found several messages from my mom and Nash, and the gist I was getting was that Tristan had told at least my mother I was staying with him for the time being to buy me time about having to explain my disappearance. How he'd gotten her to buy that explanation was a whole different matter, one I might never know the answer to.

I truly didn't know what to think of Tristan, but for now, I would keep him in the ally category. I also needed to tell him that we could cancel this new phone because I didn't need it anymore.

Easton walked back into the room and said, "No one is here, and I don't think anyone has tried to get in."

"That's a relief." I walked over to my couch with my bags, happy to finally be able to move freely in my place again. I had no idea what my first task should be now that I was back at home. Showering was on the agenda...maybe doing that and then taking a nap? Maybe going to my parents' house this evening or tomorrow?

"Bianca, there's something I need to tell you." Easton's voice broke through my thoughts.

Everything came to a halt, and I turned to face him, not sure where this was going. "What happened? I know something bad happened."

"It's not necessarily bad, but I didn't want to keep it from you."

I was afraid of what he was going to say. There were so many possibilities I wasn't sure where this was going. Potentially, it was the last thing I needed after a whirlwind trip to Italy. "What is it?" I asked, my voice slightly above a whisper.

"I reached out to Nash about your stalker," he confessed as he looked directly into my eyes. I didn't see a hint of remorse in his gaze.

A sense of betrayal washed over me. My shock and anger fought a battle within me, and I wasn't sure which emotion would win. "What? Why?"

"I wanted to use some of his resources to find out who is doing this to you. I wanted to get to the bottom of this as soon as possible, and I thought with him knowing, we would have more power at our disposal. I didn't tell him about your trip to Italy or that you were the one who leaked the information about your father though."

His logic was sound, but that wasn't the point. "But it wasn't for you to tell."

"I'm well aware," he replied calmly, his authoritative tone taking me off guard. "But I'm not going to apologize for trying to keep you safe."

I hated that his tone and the way he said it made my heart flutter. Still, I wanted to scream, but the sound didn't leave my throat. Instead, I could feel the warmth coming up my neck and to my cheeks as my eyes started to well up with frustrated tears. I couldn't help but feel violated. "You should have talked to me before you spoke to him about my battle. I trusted you!"

Easton didn't react to my outburst, nor did he lower his gaze under my glare. It was obvious he was confident he'd done the right thing. "I know, and I'm sorry I hurt you. But I thought it was best given the situation, and this was my way of showing you that you didn't need to handle any of this alone. In fact, Nash told me that he and Raven were getting similar messages."

That drew my attention slightly away from being mad at him. "Nash and Raven were getting texts too?"

Easton nodded and I was slightly annoyed that Nash hadn't told me about the messages. Then again, I hadn't told him what I was going through either. "I need to call him. Hell, I needed to even before all of this..."

I was mostly talking to myself at this point, and Easton gave me the space to do so.

"That is beside the point," I managed to say. "I appreciate what you were trying to do, but communication has to be better between us. I deserve to be informed and make my own decisions."

"If it's the difference between protecting you and putting you in harm's way, I would do this again every time. This is about protecting what is mine. *You* are mine."

The look in his eyes told me that I shouldn't doubt him. In spite of what I was feeling, I knew I couldn't afford to stay hung up on this. There was a bigger monster at hand: my stalker. The last thing I wanted to do was be pissed at someone who loved me and was doing everything in his power to help make this come to an end.

I took a deep breath as Easton spoke. "We're wondering if any of this is connected to Iris's disappearance."

Hearing Iris's name made me do a double take. "Did you find out anything about her? Is she okay?"

"As far as we know, she is, but that's all the information we have. Nash might be able to tell us more when we see him, but he was still trying to seek confirmation. At least that was the case when I spoke to him last."

"So, it's kind of still no news is good news. This doesn't make me feel any better."

"Which is a double-edged sword."

I sighed instead of saying another word because what else could I say? What else could I do that wouldn't potentially put me, Iris, or someone else I cared about in danger?

Instead, I was going to focus on what I could take care of right this second.

"Why don't we go over to Nash's place if he's available after I take a shower and nap?"

Easton gave me one nod before he said, "I think you mean after *we* take a shower."

That might have been the first time I'd seen him grin since I found out we were going to have to end our trip to Italy earlier than planned.

16

BIANCA

Easton and I rode the elevator up to Nash's apartment in silence. There hadn't been much for us to talk about. Everything hinged on what my brother had found out. Before Easton or I could knock on the door, it swung open, and Raven stood on the other side of the threshold.

Raven offered me a small smile. Her eyes flicked to Easton beside me before meeting my gaze again. "Come on in."

We followed her inside, and my gaze landed on Nash, who was busy getting some glasses out of his cabinet. He looked over his shoulder at us and placed the glasses down before walking to me.

"Bianca," Nash said, his voice filled with relief. He quickly closed the gap between us, pulling me into a hug, the likes of which had occurred less and less frequently the older we became. "How are you?"

"I'm okay. Could be better, but with everything going on, I can't ask for too much more. How are you guys? How's Mom and Dad?"

"We are fine. Mom and Dad are... coping. Barely. Dad is raging at anyone who will listen to him, and I think Mom is still in a permanent state of shock. She has this faraway look in her eyes every time I've been around her since the news broke," Nash said before he paused for a moment. "In fact, the reason why we left you alone was because Tristan told Mom that you were with him. Imagine my surprise when I get a call from Easton saying that you're with him."

"He was obviously covering for me," I blurted out.

I noticed Raven shifting out of the corner of my eye as Easton took a step toward me, so we were standing side by side. It was as if they both noticed the tension rising in the room as much as I did.

Nash's eyes narrowed at me. "Covering for you?" he repeated. "Why would he do that?"

"I..." I stammered, caught off guard by the question. It was the way he said it, accusatory, as if I'd done something bad.

I had done something, but it wasn't something wrong.

"That didn't answer my question."

It occurred to me that I didn't give a shit about keeping it a secret anymore. "I found out information on Dad regarding the escort service and gave it to Tristan. I had nothing to do with the video, but yeah. I fucking did it. It was me."

I was convinced the temperature in the room chilled several degrees when Nash's gaze turned icy. "You leaked the information about Dad to the press?" His voice was filled with disbelief. "How could you? You've not only painted a target on your back but on all of ours."

"After all the shit they've done to us? They were trying to force me into a fake marriage, for crying out loud. We are going to be fine, and it's about time he had something humble him. The only thing I feel slightly guilty about is that Mom had to find out that way, but since she was all for the arranged marriage, then she got what she deserved as well."

Anger flashed in Nash's eyes. "Do you think this is a joke? Some kind of game? I can't believe you would do something so irresponsible and reckless without even considering the consequences that would fall down on us!"

Before I could defend myself, Easton stepped between us, his body blocking me from Nash's wrath. "Enough," he said firmly, his voice surprisingly authoritative despite his usually gentle demeanor. "Both of you need to take a step back and cool down. We can't change what was done and we have a stalker on the loose."

"Easton is right," Raven said as she walked up to Nash and put a hand on his shoulder. "We are in danger, and there's no time to dwell on what happened or who did it. We need to figure out how we're going to deal with this stalker."

The tenseness in his body immediately melted away. I was happy she was able to have that effect on him. I watched as Nash looked between Raven and Easton before sighing heavily in defeat.

"You're both right," he said quietly, his gaze settling on me.

I could see that he wanted to say more, but whatever he was thinking, he kept it to himself.

My gaze shifted from Easton to Raven, a silent "thank you" passing between us for intervening when I couldn't find the words to defend myself.

"How this should have started was by Nash asking the

both of you if you wanted anything to drink. Would you like something?"

Both Easton and I shook our heads and Nash walked away from the glasses. I guessed he'd lost his desire for a drink as well.

"Do you have any information on the person who is stalking Bianca?" Easton said as he walked behind Nash. Once again, I was glad to have him here to keep us all on task.

"Not much. I contacted Parker Townsend and the weirdest thing happened," said Nash.

I glanced at Raven, who was still in the kitchen with me, and she shrugged. It seemed as if she didn't know what the hell was going on either.

"I don't understand." I'd heard the name in passing, but I didn't know exactly who he was.

Nash glanced at me before sitting down on the couch. Raven followed suit, but Easton and I remained standing. Nash cleared his throat before speaking. "He's the leader of the main Chevalier chapter in New York City. He isn't responding to any of my inquiries about the stalker. So, either he's underground and isn't reachable or..."

"He knows more than he's willing to tell about the stalker situation," Easton said, completing Nash's sentence.

"Are you serious?" I asked, shaking my head as if I didn't hear him correctly. "If this is true, why would the Chevaliers want to have someone following me?"

"Your guess is as good as mine," Nash replied. "But we need to consider all our options here, and the fact that head-quarters has suddenly gone radio silent is suspicious as hell."

"So, what do we do now?" I asked, rubbing my temple.

The beginnings of a headache were starting to form and wouldn't do me any good in this situation.

"We keep investigating in any way we can," Nash said firmly. "And we watch our backs. I know I shouldn't, given everything that has happened, but for them to be nonresponsive on this doesn't sit well with me."

"How convenient that they've been silent about Iris as well."

I turned to look at Easton and nodded. He was right. It was too convenient to be a coincidence. From what I knew, every move they made was calculated and deliberate and you wouldn't know they were involved in something until they wanted you to know. The silence and having Iris kidnapped by Soren Grant made me wonder if this was their sign. If this was letting us know that it was their power play of sorts.

What the hell was this all about?

"We need a plan," I said as I met my brother's gaze. "This might sound foolish, but is there a way we can take them on? Force their hand or something?"

The grave look on Nash's face told me all I needed to know. Easton walked up to me and threw an arm around my waist and tucked me into his body.

Nash briefly glared at Easton and his arm placement before speaking. "Even with me as leader of the Brentson University Chapter of this organization, it doesn't mean I know how powerful they are. I couldn't even tell you every member of the Chevaliers, and I know that is done by design."

"You mean they don't want one person to have too much power?" I didn't know how much Nash was willing to spill, but given the fact they might be targeting me, I didn't know how deep his loyalty ran at the moment.

Nash nodded. "We have to tread very carefully. Because it could become a matter of life or death. Actually, there is no doubt in my mind that it will lead to that if we aren't careful."

My eyes widened in shock before it sank in. Nash shared a look with Easton, and it was then I realized he wasn't talking about my death. He was referring to his and Easton's if they were caught going against the Chevaliers.

Fuck. This was so scary. "And Parker now knows you know about what is going on with me."

Nash nodded, but this time Raven spoke. "But we're assuming that this is the Chevaliers. What if it isn't? I'm not leaning one way or the other, but we seem transfixed on only one option."

She'd made an excellent point.

"Then, at some point soon, the Chevaliers will be ready to move on whoever is stalking Bianca. But if it isn't one of our own, they'd continue to be radio silent, and then it will more than likely be the best man or people win."

That forced me to do a double take. "Do you think it could be more than one person?"

"I don't know, but I also wouldn't be quick to assume that this is the workings of just one person if they are, indeed, a Chevalier."

My heart felt as if it were pounding against my ribs as I replayed Nash's ominous words in my head. Life or death. More than one person. The threat did nothing but increase the fear I'd already had. But it wasn't just my own and Iris's lives that I feared for now. It was also Nash's and Easton's. I could see it in their eyes when they met across the room.

There was a shared understanding of what they were potentially getting into, but there was also determination. The reality of what would happen if they defended me against my stalker or stalkers if they were indeed Chevaliers, had set in. These two men were ready to risk everything to protect me. It was both heartwarming and terrifying at the same time.

The silence that followed between us was deafening. We were stuck in our own thoughts as the sun began to set. While we weren't any closer to finding out who my stalker was, at least it seemed that we were all in this together, and we wouldn't be going down without a fight.

17

BIANCA

The next evening, I was in the passenger seat of Easton's car, pulling up to my parents' home. Through the living room window, I could see my parents' silhouettes. By their hand motions, they were arguing again, even though I couldn't make out what was being said.

Easton parked in their driveway and shut off the engine. Silence fell between us as we sat there, staring at the house before us. My childhood home, which had been filled with some bittersweet memories and was now tainted by the toxicity of my parents' desire for power and my father's indiscretions.

I took a shaky breath, and Easton reached over and grabbed my hand, sensing the turmoil that was going through me. I held on to his as if it was my only hope of surviving. "I don't know if I can do this," I whispered.

"You can do this, and you don't have to go in there alone," he said softly. "I'll go in there with you."

"I think this is something I need to take care of alone."

"Then I'll wait out here for you."

"Are you sure?"

Easton turned and looked at me. "Of course I am."

"Thank you."

I stepped out of the car before he could respond and shifted into the cool night air. I closed the car door behind me before I walked toward the house. Was I ready to confront whatever was happening inside? No, but I was still going to do this.

I used my key to unlock the front door and walked inside to find my parents in the living room, as expected. But the sight before me was somewhat shocking, to say the least.

Dad was disheveled in a way I'd never seen him before. His bloodshot eyes were narrowed in anger. An empty bottle of whiskey sat on the coffee table beside him.

Mom looked worse for wear as well. Her makeup was smeared under her eyes from what I assumed was from crying.

She looked over at me before she threw her hands up and yelled, "How could you fucking do this to me? After everything I've done for you! The sacrifices I made so that you could succeed and make your dream a reality. This is how you repay me?"

"Oh, spare me the martyr act," Dad scoffed, words slightly slurred. "You've never sacrificed or wanted for anything since I married you."

I flinched at the venom in his tone. They were at each other's throats, tearing apart at the seams.

I was the cause of this. I was the reason why the facade that we put out into the world had been shattered and ripped to shreds.

While there was some guilt still, there was something else there as well. Peace. I was at peace with what I'd done.

I cleared my throat, stepping farther into the room. "Mom. Dad. Stop."

Dad still hadn't noticed I was there even after I spoke, but Mom was more than aware.

Mom grabbed a vase from one of her end tables and threw it. It went flying across the room in my father's direction. He managed to dodge it, and the vase shattered against the wall. I immediately recognized it as the vase my mother had told me they'd received as a wedding gift.

"Hey! I fucking said to stop!" I shouted, tired of the scene unfolding in front of me.

They both froze in place, and it took a few more seconds before they both turned to face me. Shock flickered over their faces before they looked away from me and each other.

Silence filled the room, and I was grateful for it. It helped lessen the tension vibrating between the two of them and gave me an opportunity to think.

I shook my head as I took in the scene before me. "How did we get here?" I whispered. "When did our family fall apart?"

My father's jaw clenched, but he refused to look at me. However, my mother lifted her gaze to meet mine as tears fell down her cheeks.

It was obvious how much she was hurting, and even after all she'd done to me, I was hurting in a way too.

"Dad, why don't you cool off in your office?"

My father gave a curt nod in my general direction before leaving the room. He didn't even look at me as he passed by.

I shifted my gaze back to my mother, who was now

standing in front of me. Everything about her seemed to show she was broken and defeated.

She and I rarely got along, but I opened my arms and allowed her to step into them. She immediately broke down, sobbing into my coat. I didn't say a word, letting her have the opportunity to express her emotions instead of trying to start a conversation.

Part of me wanted to be as vicious to her as she was to me, but right now, I couldn't be. For some reason, I wanted to be there for her, even if it was temporary, because of the pain she was currently living with.

It took her some time before she was able to calm down. When she pulled away from me to wipe her tears away, I said, "Let me help you clean up this mess."

"You don't have to."

"It's fine. I promise."

My mom nodded, and together, we started picking up the pieces of the shattered vase. I left the room briefly to get a broom, a dustpan, and a garbage bag. We worked mostly in silence, choosing to stay transfixed in our thoughts versus making conversation with one another. Once the mess was cleaned up, I walked over to one of the windows in the living room and looked outside. Easton was still sitting there in his SUV.

He hadn't left.

"Bianca," my mom said as I quickly turned toward her when she called my name. "I'm so sorry. I never meant for things to end up this way."

"We never expect things to go wrong when we're flying high... but they do," I said. "And now there's no going back."

No response came for a few moments, and I hoped that was her taking the time to truly listen to the words I'd said.

So, I kept talking. "Mom, I came home to talk to you."

"Oh really? What's going on? I am glad you did come over, although I'm not happy you had to see your parents fighting. I assume Tristan has kept you informed about what is going on?"

This was it. The moment of truth.

"I knew about it, and it had nothing to do with Tristan."

Mom's eyes widened at my admission. "Did the press come to you for comment? Why didn't you tell us?"

"No one came to me. I went to them."

My mother blinked at me once and then twice as she tried to process what I'd said.

"You went to the press? Without telling us first!?" Her voice rose with each word.

I cringed at the sound. However, this was what I was expecting would happen.

I took a deep breath before I replied. "Yes, I did. I didn't have a choice because I refused to marry Tristan."

"But why didn't you come to me first?" she asked me. "We could have found another way to handle it. We could have thought of a solution before going to the press."

I folded my arms across my chest. "Would you have listened to me if I had told you the truth? I think you would have doubled down on me marrying Tristan to keep it quiet. This family was built on everyone only looking out for themselves. I just carried on the tradition."

The silence that followed was deafening. I could see the emotion playing across my mom's face, and I wondered if she finally understood why I'd done what I had done.

I could see my mom's face soften as she thought about what I had said. What my father had done was horrible, and my mom shouldn't be blamed for him cheating on her. But she'd played a role in creating this monster by cosigning this fake engagement.

My mom rubbed a hand down her face as I saw that tears were starting to form again. "You're right. You're absolutely right."

Her revelation slammed into me as if she'd slapped me.

She let out a deep breath and said, "This family has enough secrets that have been buried for far too long."

I could agree with her about that. When my phone vibrated in my coat pocket, I took it out and noticed a text from Easton.

Easton: Is everything alright?

"Is that Tristan?"

I looked up at my mom and gave her a small smile. "It's not. I wasn't with Tristan at all."

Confusion covered her face. "I... I don't understand."

"Tristan covered for me. I wasn't anywhere near him over the last week or so. I was alone, and then Easton joined me."

My mother's brows shot up and she said, "Easton?"

"He's been absolutely wonderful. He found out where I was and immediately flew to be with me. I loved spending time with him. Hell, I love him."

"I didn't know any of that."

She slowly nodded and I could see understanding on her face. There was a long stretch of silence where all my mother could do was look at her feet. I wondered if she was going to say something else.

She took a deep breath and rolled her shoulders back. Remnants of the politician's wife were starting to resurface, and I wondered if that, too, was just a mask she decided to hide behind. Then she said, "Why don't you invite him in?"

I raised an eyebrow at her, but she gestured to my phone. I quickly typed up a message.

> Me: It's something. My mom asked that you come in.

As I was putting my phone away, Mom said, "I'm so sorry for my part in creating this fake engagement and trying to run your life. We shouldn't have taken things as far as we did, and we should have found a way out of any mess ourselves. One of the promises I made to myself when your father ran for mayor was we wouldn't do anything that would jeopardize yours or Nash's happiness, and we failed."

I wanted to believe every word she said, but I was still skeptical. It all sounded good, but I didn't trust that she'd done a one-eighty within the last couple of minutes. But there was a small glimmer of hope.

When there was a knock on the door, both my mother and I walked to the hallway. I briefly looked back at my father's closed office door before I turned to my mother, who was about to open the front door.

My mother opened the door, and we found Easton standing there with his hands at his sides. He had a determined look on his face, but when his eyes reached mine, he smiled.

"Hi," he said as he stepped through the doorway.

My mom opened her arms and when Easton stepped into them, I heard her whisper, "Thank you."

Easton pulled away and gave me a confused look and asked, "You're welcome, but I'm not sure what for?"

"For being there with my daughter when she needed someone the most." She turned to Easton and said, "How about we have a small dinner party tomorrow? Just us, your father, and we can invite Nash and Raven as well. Maybe, we can smooth things over with... everyone."

I raised an eyebrow at her. "Is that okay with you given what just happened?"

I watched as the mask shifted back onto my mother's face. She was back to being the politician's wife. "Yes. Everything will be fine."

I wasn't sure if that was a good idea, but I did want to give her a chance. "If Easton's schedule is clear, I think we can make it."

"There's nothing pressing on it."

My mom clapped her hands together and said, "Excellent. I'll take care of everything, and we should be ready to go by seven."

I didn't know what tomorrow's dinner would bring, but I suspected it would be anything but normal.

18

BIANCA

I played with the necklace Easton had given me as a way to calm my nerves. To say I wasn't nervous about tonight would be a lie.

It was the evening after I'd gone to my mother's house and sort of cleared the air. But that didn't mean I wasn't worried about being in my father's presence again.

"What are you thinking about?"

I looked over my shoulder and found Easton pulling his sweater over his torso, covering the six-pack I'd come to adore.

"I'm worried about tonight."

He stepped behind me and placed a gentle kiss on my shoulder. He then wrapped his arms around me, pulling me close. His arms provided security and warmth, making me wish that we could stay like this forever.

"It's going to be alright," he whispered in my ear as his hold on me tightened. "I will make sure that no one does anything to upset you."

"I don't want you to fight all of my battles for me, Easton."

He loosened his grip on me so that he could turn me around. Once we were face to face, he put his hand under my jaw and lifted it, forcing me to look him right in the eye. "I'm not fighting any of your battles. I'm standing in your corner, providing the support you need to get what you want."

I gave him a small smile as he tucked a piece of my hair behind my ear. Before I could say another word, he spoke again. "That doesn't mean I won't fuck someone up for you though."

I chuckled. "Please try to keep your hands to yourself when it comes to my father."

"It depends on how he treats you. If he doesn't give me a reason to put my hands on him, then we're all good."

His words were reassuring enough for me, and I leaned up to give him a kiss on the lips. We stayed like that for a few minutes before we broke apart. If we didn't get out of my apartment, we were going to be late.

Easton grabbed his coat and keys while I put on mine and grabbed my purse. We rushed to his SUV to stave off the cold, and all the while, I tried to keep my nerves in check. I took a deep breath before getting into the vehicle.

It was going to be fine.

As we drove toward my parents' house, Easton held my hand in an attempt to calm my nerves. I wasn't sure how much it was working, but I appreciated the attempt. I watched as the streetlights flickered and night began to fall. When we drove down the lit-up driveway, my eyes were drawn to the other cars that were parked closer to the house. I noticed Nash's car, indicating that he and Raven had already arrived. Easton turned off the engine and glanced over at me.

"Are you ready?"

"As ready as I'll ever be," I said, and I meant every word.

He gave me a small head nod before he opened his door and got out of the vehicle. He quickly came around to open my door, and once I was out, he put a hand on the small of my back, guiding me to my parents' front door.

Easton did the honors and knocked on the door, and while we waited for someone to open it, my stomach twisted into a tight knot. It would have been quicker for me to pull out my key and unlock the door, but the thought of even trying to find my keys in my purse was daunting at the moment. How was I going to be able to sit there and eat dinner if I felt as if I was going to vomit?

Suddenly, the door swung open and both Easton and I were face to face with my mother once more. She gave me and then Easton a small smile, and I could see that it didn't reach her eyes at all. While she looked perfectly presentable, much like she did whenever they were hosting a party, there was sadness in her eyes, and I knew what had put it there.

"Please, come on in," Mom said, and we followed her lead.

The first thing that greeted me was the scent of roasted ham floating through the house. I was amazed at how, even though everything was decorated for the holidays and should be a time for joy and festivities, my stomach churned with each step I took.

Easton and I quickly hung up our coats in the hallway closet, and it seemed as if we'd made it just in time because, in the dining room, an elaborate feast was spread across the table. My father was sitting at one end of the table and my mother walked to the other end instead of taking her seat near him. I silently applauded her. For a woman who was obsessed with appearances, she'd shown, in a small way, she wasn't happy being anywhere near her husband.

Nash and Raven were seated next to each other on one side, which meant that either Easton or I had to sit next to my father on the other side. As if he knew or sensed my discomfort, Easton pulled out the chair two down from my dad, putting me between Easton and my mother versus me having to sit next to my father.

I sighed and slid into my seat, the tension in the room thick enough to cut with the knives at our place settings. We were all here together again, but everyone knew the perfect world that had been created for us had been shattered into a billion pieces.

"Now that everyone is here, why don't we dig in?" My mother's falsely cheerful voice cut through the silence.

I looked at Nash and all he did was give me a head nod. With that, the feast began. Forks clinked against plates as polite conversation began to fill the awkwardness I was sure the majority of us felt.

Everyone tried to carefully avoid the elephant in the room. As far as holiday dinners went, this could have been worse, outside of my father's scandal, of course. Maybe if we hurried up and got through dinner, then we could leave, and I wouldn't have to think about being back here for a while.

That was a whole lot of wishful thinking.

I stared down at my plate, picking at the food I had no appetite for and wished I were anywhere but here. Easton must have noticed my mood because his hand landed on my knee, where he gave it a squeeze. I gave him a small smile as Nash cleared his throat, drawing the attention back to him.

"Easton, are you dying to get back on the field as much as

I am?"

A slow, knowing smile spread across Easton's face. "More than you know," he replied as he put his fork down and leaned back in his chair. "I look forward to the adrenaline rush and the crowd cheering us on. There is nothing quite like it."

"I have a good feeling that next season will be even better."

"I have no doubts."

I watched as the two nodded at each other. Not only did they share a brotherhood with one another with their Chevalier memberships, but football was a huge bond they shared as well. It was more than just a game for them. I assumed that no matter what was happening off the field in their lives, they could always count on each other when it came to leaving everything on the field.

Although I didn't have much to add to the conversation, I was grateful for my brother and my—I wasn't exactly sure what Easton was to me—for trying to keep the light conversation going. It was a way to avoid all the awkwardness that surrounded us, which made me wish the ground would open up and swallow me whole.

"Do you all have any plans for winter break?" my mom asked when the chatter about football died down and the silence became too much.

"Nash and I were thinking of going to Vail to go skiing," Raven chimed in.

"That would be really nice," my mom said as she turned to me.

I wanted to blurt out that I'd already been out of the country, but the majority of the people at the table had no idea about that. Instead, I glanced at Easton before I said, "We haven't discussed it yet, but I'm sure we'll think of something."

Well, that was before my father decided to utter his first words of the night.

"Well, it must be nice to have plans for the holidays that don't involve trying to salvage your career." The sarcasm dripped over his words, and I hated him for it.

The table grew quiet, the previous friendly chatter replaced with an uncomfortable tension. I couldn't help but wonder if Mom or Nash had told him that I'd been the one who leaked the information about him to the press.

Dad's eyes shifted between Nash and my mother before he landed on me.

"Van, stop it."

I looked over, somewhat in shock that my mother had spoken up.

Instead of listening to his wife, my father slammed his fist down on the table, making me jump. "Your fucking daughter disappeared when her family was in a crisis and shows back up a week later. What kind of shit is that?"

"Don't speak to her like that or about me that way," I said before I could stop myself. The anger had grown within me so swiftly I couldn't control it or my words.

"Excuse me?" My father started to stand up before he continued. "Do you want to say that again?"

"You heard me just fine, *Dad*."

"Bianca, if you don't—"

That was all it took for me to snap. I stood up too and yelled, "If I don't, what? Bow to your every need and keep my thoughts to myself? You want everyone to follow your lead and do what you want them to do, but that's not how this world works. You fucked up. You were the one who was caught cheating on your wife of twenty-seven years and embarrassing our family. It was all your fucking fault, so frankly, I don't give a shit about what you have to say because it is meaningless. It's all pure bullshit and you know it."

With how red my father had turned, I was convinced he was going to launch himself over the table to fight me. But before he could think about doing anything, Easton jumped up too, putting himself between me and my father.

"Bianca, we're going to head out. And Van, you're going to sit back in your seat and enjoy your meal and pretend as if you didn't even think about striking your daughter," Easton said firmly, daring anyone to doubt him. As he clenched and unclenched his fist, I knew he was barely hanging onto his self-control and was liable to throw away his promise to me.

I stared at the two men in front of me before I grabbed my purse and walked out of the room and grabbed my coat. As I finished putting it on, Easton, my mom, Nash, and Raven joined me in the foyer.

My mom pulled me into a hug without saying a word, and I was left standing there for a few moments in confusion and didn't move a muscle. It took a few seconds for my brain to compute before I was able to wrap my arms around her and give her a hug back.

"We'll talk later," Nash said.

I gave him a small head nod. When I turned to look back at Easton, he had his coat on and held out his hand for me to hold. With our hands intertwined, we walked out of my parents' home together and into the night air. It was the first time I'd been able to breathe clearly all night.

19

BIANCA

The front door slammed shut behind us. I could have sworn the sound echoed through the neighborhood, even though I was sure the noise only sounded loud to those of us who were near it. As Easton guided me to his SUV, it felt as if we'd only just arrived seconds ago. Hell, I doubted we'd been here longer than twenty minutes.

Once we were on the road, neither one of us said a word because the tension from dinner hung between us as we processed what we'd just experienced.

"Shit, Bianca," Easton muttered under his breath. "That was... intense."

"Intense doesn't even begin to cover it," I said, gripping the door handle as if I could somehow escape this whole fucked-up situation. I wished I'd been mentally more prepared for the heated words that were thrown at me just minutes ago.

I stared out the window, watching the scenery passing me

by when I noticed something. The route he was taking wouldn't take me back to my apartment.

"Where are we going?" I asked and I somewhat patiently waited for an answer.

Easton glanced at me, but his main focus was on the road. He didn't say anything for a moment. The only sound that could be heard was the humming of the engine.

"Easton. Where are you taking me?" My patience was almost nonexistent at this point.

"Somewhere you can have some space after what just happened," he replied.

"Fine," I sighed at his non-answer. But it was anything but fine, really, and Easton apparently knew that as well.

"Alright, you want to know where we're going?" Easton's voice was calm, but I could hear the underlying annoyance in his tone.

I didn't know if that was directed at me or because of what my father had almost done.

"We're going to my parents' house."

"Your parents' house?" My heart skipped a beat. Was this what it felt like to be punched in the face? Why would he take me there? "Why?"

"To give you some downtime and some festive cheer after that debacle. You don't need to worry because they already love you, Bianca." He glanced over at me again. "You don't have to worry about anything."

"Um..." My voice trailed off as all my emotions took over. "Do you really think that's a good idea? Because I'm not so sure it is."

"Trust me, okay?" His hand reached over and grabbed mine. "You already know each other."

"Yes, but that was in my capacity as the mayor's daughter. Not being their son's…" I couldn't think of how to describe us since we hadn't discussed a label for whatever this was.

"What do you want to be to me, Bianca?"

"This conversation wasn't on my bingo card tonight."

That made Easton chuckle. "Were any of tonight's events on it?"

"I mean, I did expect my father to still be pissed about his private affairs being made public. I didn't expect to snap at him about how he was treating us, but I can be a wildcard at times. Heading to your parents' and you asking me how I wanted to define 'us' most definitely wasn't."

"Honest answer. I like that. But I already knew you were mine the moment I met you, even if it took a while for me to pull my head out of my own ass. Whatever you want to call yourself, whether it's my girlfriend, my lover, my everything, it doesn't matter. All that matters is that you're mine."

"Fuck," I muttered, but it was obvious he'd heard me because he'd turned to glance at me before focusing his attention back on the road. His words had shaken me to my core.

I agreed with him. He was mine and I was his.

"You can introduce me as your girlfriend then. That's probably the easiest."

"That's what we'll do then." He brought my hand to his lips. "It's going to be fine. I promise."

"Okay. It's going to be fine," I said as I turned my attention toward the window once more.

The drive was a blur of darkness and light. Night had fallen in Brentson, but the town was lit up by shop signs, streetlights, and car lights. I tried to focus on the soft music that Easton had turned up slightly on the SUV's sound system.

"We are almost there," Easton said, as his hand still held mine.

I knew we were getting close because we'd left the city limits and were now on the outskirts of town and I'd heard that was where Easton's parents had purchased their house a couple of years ago.

"Look, there it is," he said.

I looked up and found a mansion coming into view around a bend in the road. Before we even got up close to the house, I could see the time and care that was given to the property even though it was winter. The house looked to be mostly brick, and it sat on an expansive piece of land. There looked to be a garden I was sure contained lots of flowers when they were in season.

"Come on, let's go inside."

He parked the car in the circular driveway, and we left the vehicle. Easton held out his hand once more for me to grab, and together, we walked up to the front door.

The foyer was stunning and more spacious than my childhood home. As I tried to study my new environment further, someone spoke.

"Easton, what are you doing here?"

Both Easton and I turned to see his mother, Amelia, walking down a hallway.

"Mom," Easton greeted her, his voice warm and tender.

Amelia reached us and wrapped him in a tight embrace. "I haven't seen you since before you left for Italy," she said.

I bit my lip. The reason why he'd left the United States

was because of me. The two of them stayed like that for a few minutes, and when she released him, she turned to me.

"Ah, Bianca," she said as her eyes lit up. "It's lovely to see you again." She hugged me, and the faded scent of her floral perfume was warm and inviting, just like her.

I hugged her back, immediately feeling welcomed into her home.

Easton took off his coat and I followed suit.

"Can I get you both something to eat or drink?" Amelia asked, leading us down the hallway that she came from. We walked into a spacious kitchen that looked like it belonged on the cover of a magazine. "We have a chef, of course, but I can still whip up a little something."

She opened the fridge, stocked to the brim with food, and started pulling out ingredients. I glanced over at Easton, who was watching his mother with amusement and adoration.

Easton gave me a playful smirk when he looked over at me. I rolled my eyes, but I couldn't help the small, relieved smile that appeared on my face.

It took some time, but Amelia made some hot chocolate and poured it into four mugs. Its warmth and sweetness were perfect for this chilly evening.

"Thank you," I replied, taking a small sip. "It's delicious."

"You're very welcome," Amelia said. "I made some for Oliver too, because it's one of his favorite treats in the winter."

I continued to nurse my hot chocolate when the sound of footsteps approaching from the hallway caught my attention.

"Ah, there you are, sweetheart!" Easton's father, Oliver, strolled into the kitchen. He gave his wife a warm smile before he clapped his son on the shoulder, then turned his attention to me. "Bianca, welcome to our home. I hope the Amalfi Coast was lovely."

"Thanks," I mumbled as I took another sip from my mug. I could feel my cheeks growing warm.

"Oliver, Easton and Bianca decided to stop by tonight, but I'm not sure how long they are staying," Amelia said.

"I'm not sure how long we are either, to be honest," Easton chimed in. "I just wanted to bring Bianca here for a break."

"How about we get some snacks and watch a movie in the home theater?" Oliver offered.

"Sounds good to me," I replied truthfully. Anything was better than what I'd been through tonight.

"Great! I'll go set things up." With one last smile, he left the kitchen and disappeared down the hall.

"Should we make some popcorn?" Amelia asked once her husband was out of earshot.

"That would be perfect," Easton said as he pulled me close.

"I'd love some too," I said, enjoying the feel of Easton's arms wrapped around me.

We helped Amelia make enough popcorn for the four of us and then left the kitchen to head into the basement. The home theater had plush leather seats and wall-to-wall screens. I sank into one of the chairs and sighed. This was relaxing.

"Any preferences?" Oliver asked as he glanced at me. He was standing in front of an impressive collection of DVDs. "We also have access to all of the streaming platforms."

"Whatever you guys want to watch is fine with me," I said, not trusting myself to make a decision.

"Let's see…" Amelia said, scanning the titles before she settled on something. "How about this one?"

"Perfect." Oliver set the system up and dimmed the lights.

Easton sat down next to me as the movie began. As it went on, I tried to focus on the story unfolding, but my mind was still on what happened at my parents'. As I was grabbing a piece of popcorn, Easton's hand slid over and grabbed mine. The warmth of Easton's hand made me grin.

The movie ended and the lights slowly brightened. Easton squeezed my hand and I turned to look at him.

"Do you want to see the rest of the house?" he asked.

"Sure," I replied, curious about what the rest of the house looked like. Also, it would be nice to get some alone time with him.

"We'll see you both later," Oliver said.

Once we left the basement, Easton led me through the mansion, pointing out rooms filled with expensive art pieces and furniture. We finally reached his bedroom, tucked away on the other side of the house. He turned on a lamp that was on a nightstand near his bed, basking the whole room in a warm glow.

The walls were painted a light gray, and a king-size bed dominated the room. The comforter was a dark blue and the rest of his linens seemed to be white. In one corner of the room, there were some weights that were collecting dust. In another, there was a cabinet that contained football trophies I assumed were from high school.

"Wow," I said as I looked around the room. "This is nice."

"I could give you a tour of every area of my room and show you how nice it really is."

As I looked at him, Easton caught my face in his hands and pressed his lips against mine.

20

EASTON

Having my lips on her again was magical. Her body's response to mine was all I could think about. I wrapped my hands around her waist and brought her closer to me. The heat and desire burning between us was almost unbearable, but I hoped it was never extinguished.

My hands made their way to her head and got tangled in her hair. Flashes of me defending her against her father shone through. Seeing the hurt look that quickly turned to shock when he acted as if he might launch himself at her did nothing but enrage me.

But I tamped down my anger at her father because I didn't want to take it out on her.

Bianca broke away from me and said, "What's wrong?"

I caressed her cheek as I looked into her eyes. "What do you mean?"

"You growled while you were kissing me."

"It was nothing."

Bianca rolled her beautiful eyes. "That's a lie."

"Couldn't it have just been that you bring out my wild side?"

Her lips twitched in response. "I doubt that, but I wouldn't mind exploring that side with you."

"Are you sure?"

"Do it."

"Do you want to pick a safe word? Or should I give you one?"

"Safe word?"

I brushed her hair back from her face. "I want you to feel completely safe always, but especially when we're together. If there's something I do that you don't like, I want you to let me know by saying a word that means stop."

Bianca nodded slowly. "How about crown?"

I glanced at the necklace I bought her and said, "Excellent choice."

I didn't give her a chance to respond because my lips were back on her. This time, my hands made their way to her neck, rubbing my fingers along the necklace. I gently ran both hands down her throat before making my way back to her hair and pulling on it hard.

Her gasp of surprise was music to my ears. I couldn't help but stare at the column of her throat as she swallowed. She didn't know what I was going to do next, and I loved it.

I used my free hand to lift up the long-sleeve shirt she'd decided to wear tonight and tossed it to the side, exposing the red lace bra I'd watched her put on earlier. I yanked it down, freeing one of her breasts for my eyes to feast on. She made a move to cover her exposed breast, but I pulled her arm away, allowing myself to take in the image in front of me before I bent down to take her nipple into my mouth.

"Are your parents going to hear us?"

Hearing her speak instead of just making sounds took me by surprise. "No," I rushed out. "Their bedroom is on the other side of the house."

I teased her with my tongue and used my teeth to tug on it gently. I could feel her body trying to get closer to me in response, heard the low moans coming from her lips, and couldn't help but smile.

I yanked the other cup down and moved to her other breast, teasing it in the same manner. Her groans grew louder as her fingers made their way into my hair, anchoring me to her chest. She hissed when I bit her a little harder, but she didn't say her safe word and the hiss turned into a moan just as I knew it would.

I took my time exploring every inch of her chest, leaving kisses and licks as I went. While my mouth was occupied with one breast, I made sure the other one had the attention of my hand. Feeling her squirm against me was a treat, one I'd never get tired of.

When I was done feasting on her breasts, I pulled her flush against me, her lips just inches away from mine. I ground my hips into her and said, "Do you feel what you do to me, princess?"

All she could do was nod rapidly, and I couldn't deny how good it felt to leave her speechless.

I grabbed her hand and walked her over to my bed. I positioned her so that her back was facing the bed and left an earth-shattering kiss on her lips once more. When she pulled apart from me to take a quick breath, I took a small step back and said, "Take off your pants, socks, and shoes."

"And my underwear too?"

I raised an eyebrow at her. "Did I ask you to do that?"

She bit the corner of her lip but didn't say another word. Instead, she quickly unbuttoned her jeans and slid them down her legs, making quick work of removing her shoes, socks, and pants.

"Good job, princess," I said, and I watched her eyes darken with desire. However, I didn't give her much opportunity to process what I'd said.

I quickly turned her around and laid my hand on her back, forcing her to bend at the waist. I walked around to the side of my bed and back to get an eyeful of her breasts hanging out of her bra cups before I stood behind that beautiful ass of hers. And I couldn't be more thankful that she'd decided to wear a thong today.

Adrenaline shot through me as I waited to make my move. She didn't know what I was going to do or when I was going to do it. All she could do was stand there and take whatever I was about to give her.

She groaned right after my hand landed on her ass.

I squeezed it gently before running my fingertips across her skin, then I slapped her other ass cheek.

I repeated my actions a couple of times and enjoyed the way her ass was turning pink under my touch. Then I leaned forward and pressed a little kiss on the small of her back and grabbed the fabric of her thong with my teeth. She gasped and looked over her shoulder as I used my teeth to pull the thong down her legs, and she quickly stepped out of it.

I ran a finger down her seam until I reached her pussy. But that was where I stopped.

"I love how wet you get when I spank your ass."

I looked up to catch her reaction and noticed that she was biting her lip once more. "Are you holding back on me?"

Bianca nodded quickly. "I'm still worried your parents are going to come to this side of the house and check on us."

Her concern made me chuckle. I used my other hand to grab her blonde hair and pulled. "Trust me. They know we're fucking right now. So, all I want to hear you saying is what I'm doing to you and how close I am to making you come."

"Shit," she said out loud.

I took that as my sign to continue.

Her body was nothing but tension as I continued to tease her by not doing what she wanted. My finger remained at her pussy, but I didn't play with her clit or enter her. At least, not yet.

It was obvious she was waiting for something more, but I couldn't help but tease her a bit more first.

"How badly do you want me to finger you, princess?"

She took in a deep breath and said, "More than anything else in the world."

"I'm going to need you to do better than that. I want you to beg me to fuck you in any way I see fit."

"And if I don't?"

"All of this ends right now."

There was silence between us as she thought about what I said. I wondered if she was going to use her safe word.

"Please," she begged, her voice cracking with the need for me to take her. "Please fuck me."

"Say it again."

When she did, I growled. "That's what I like to hear."

I finally allowed my finger to enter her, and as it sank into her body, I couldn't wait for it to be my cock.

I started off slow until I was sure she was used to my finger, and I could sense that she was getting frustrated with how slow things were going. I decided to give in to both of our desires and increased my pace tenfold.

"F-fuck," she said as she looked over her shoulder to see what she could of what I was doing to her. Her body shifted and swayed as I used my finger to pound into her, riding this feeling as she got closer and closer to an orgasm.

I slapped her ass again and she yelped, this time much louder than she'd done previously. When her moans increased in volume and intensity, I knew she was close, and she couldn't take much more.

I licked her pussy, and that was the flame that set everything off.

She screamed out in pleasure as her orgasm hit her hard. Her body shook as her fingers gripped the comforter tightly. I continued to thrust my finger into her, allowing her to ride out the wave. Bianca fell slightly forward as her breathing turned heavy and ragged.

But this wasn't over.

I quickly rid myself of all my clothes, giving Bianca an opportunity to recover.

But the recovery time wasn't long.

I pulled her toward me slightly and used my foot to separate her feet more, forcing her legs wider. Then I sank into her without preamble.

There was nothing like her tight walls surrounding my cock.

My thrusts left no room for either of us to think. All that mattered was fucking her.

"This is what... I wanted," she managed to get out. "I love this."

I smiled before I found myself staring at her ass and where we were so intimately connected. Watching my cock slide in and out of her was mesmerizing, to say the least, and was a sight I'd never get tired of.

I continued to slam into her hard and deep as she continued to voice her pleasure.

But that wasn't enough.

I wanted more.

I reached around her body and began to massage her clit as I kept pounding into her. I was pretty sure she would have fallen over if I hadn't been using my other hand to hold onto her waist.

"Easton," my name from her lips sounded clipped as if she couldn't finish the last syllable because of the pleasure coursing through her body. I was driving her wild and enjoying every minute of it.

My own body began to follow the same trend and grew tense as I could feel myself growing close as well.

I adjusted my positioning so that I was standing up again and both hands were on her waist. I slammed into her as if it would be the last thing I would do on this planet, fucking her as if my life depended on it.

To me, it felt as if it did, and I had no regrets.

Her screams filled my mind as I watched her sail away, caught in the ecstasy that her second orgasm was giving her.

However, I didn't let off on the brutal pace I'd set. I was determined to join her on the other side of my own climax and help her ride out hers.

I squeezed my eyes shut as I felt myself getting close. This was it.

When I followed her over the edge, I could have sworn I saw stars. I undid Bianca's bra completely and slowly let her go. She collapsed on the bed.

"That was incredible," Bianca said. She removed her bra slowly and tossed it over the edge of the bed before turning onto her back.

"I have to agree with that assessment." I stood up and walked to my bathroom.

"Where are you going? I want to cuddle."

I chuckled at her half whine, half plea. "I need to get us both cleaned up before we can cuddle. Then we'll decide if we want to stay here for the night."

"I like that, but it doesn't matter to me."

I couldn't control my tired grin. *All that mattered was that she was here with me.*

21

BIANCA

I unlocked the door of Easton's SUV as the rain that started as a drizzle picked up. It was back to reality, I thought as I glanced up at my apartment building.

I turned my attention to the man beside me and said, "Thanks for the ride."

I smiled at Easton, who was sitting in the driver's seat. It was the next morning, and Easton and I had decided to stay at his parents' home, where we enjoyed a lovely breakfast prepared by their chef.

It almost made me wish we didn't have to leave. Being around his parents for several hours over the course of the last couple of days had shown me what it would be like to be with a family who wasn't built on pure dysfunction.

"It won't take me longer than thirty minutes to wrap up things at my apartment and then I'll be back over here."

Easton's words brought me out of the thoughts I was having about my experience at his parents'. "That should be fine."

"Are you okay with going up to your apartment by yourself?"

I couldn't help but roll my eyes. "If he didn't try to access my apartment while we were in Europe, then I highly doubt he tried to this morning or last night. I'll keep my cell phone out in my hand in case I need it."

"Excellent. Now kiss me."

"You could ask nicely, Easton."

"I'm making a demand. Kiss me."

I shivered from his words and the tone of his voice. It reminded me of the adventure we'd had the night before when he'd asked me to beg him before he would fuck me. Something deep within me knew I wouldn't deny him a kiss.

So I didn't.

Our lips met and I sighed into our kiss. It wasn't as intense as our kisses last night, but I loved it all the same.

Easton pulled away first and said, "I hate that I cut our kiss short, but I want to get back here as soon as I can."

"I want that too," I said as I opened the door and was greeted by a rush of cold air.

"Hey, Bianca."

I turned to look back at Easton and said, "Yes?"

"I love you."

I was still getting used to hearing him say those words. "I love you too."

I stepped out of the SUV and walked to my apartment building. The quicker I took a shower and changed my clothes, the better.

I pushed open the glass door and entered the lobby of my apartment building. I was immediately greeted by a gust of warm air, and I sighed. The only thing that would be better would be the shower my body was dying to take.

"Ms. Henson."

I turned toward the voice, wondering why the person at the front desk would be calling me.

But I was wrong.

My gaze landed on Diana Caldwell. A million and a half questions flew through my head as I tried to piece together why she would be here.

"What are you doing here, Diana?" I said, harsher than necessary. I figured it was because she took me off guard. It was also a matter of me trying to mask the panic that I actually felt.

"No need to be so hostile, Bianca," she said as she stepped forward. Her heels *click-clacked* against the floor, echoing in the lobby. "I just wanted to talk to you, and I won't take up too much of your time."

"Talk?" I scoffed, crossing my arms over my chest. "What could you possibly want to talk to me about? My father's failing mayoral campaign? Shouldn't you be talking to him?"

"No. I'm talking to the Henson that I want to talk to." She sighed, and I could see she was trying to maintain her composure. After all, she was still in public, and people might recognize who she was. "Is there somewhere we can talk that is more private?"

I raised an eyebrow at her because of how suspicious I was about all of this. There was no way I was allowing her into my apartment. Hell, how had she even found out where I lived? Could she be the person who was stalking me?

I looked down at my phone and then back up at Diana as

an idea popped into my head. "Let's see if one of the conference rooms on the main floor is open and we can talk there."

It would provide the privacy she wanted, but also allow me to remain as close to being public as possible. Diana gestured for me to walk ahead, and I led us into the area where everyone who rented or owned an apartment in the building was allowed to use these rooms during preset hours. People usually used them for work meetings or calls.

Thankfully, a smaller meeting room was empty, and I held the door open as Diana joined me in the space. Black leather ergonomic chairs were placed around a conference table. A state-of-the-art flat-screen monitor was mounted on the off-white wall at one end of the room, ready for presentations or video calls. A countertop to our left held a high-end coffee machine and a variety of snacks.

We both sat down at the table at the same time, and I waited for her to speak first.

She tapped her fingertips on the table while looking around the room. She looked unsure of herself, and I couldn't help but wonder what was on her mind. If she didn't start talking soon, Easton would be back, and she would have done nothing but waste my time. And the last thing I had was time to waste, so I spoke up.

"What brings you here, Diana?" I tried my best to be nicer than I'd been when she startled me with her ambush.

"I wanted to tell you that I sent those photos of you to your father."

My blood turned cold. I wasn't sure how to react, so instead, I froze in place for a few seconds. There's no way she'd said what I thought she said. "What the hell? You can't be fucking serious."

I couldn't process what she'd just confessed to. It had been the last thing I'd been expecting her to say.

"I am," she said with a small nod. "After all, how would I know about them? The pictures were never leaked to the public."

"Was it a way for you to try to blackmail him? Pretty sure that's illegal."

Diana rolled her eyes and as I watched her slouch in her chair, I noticed she was becoming more relaxed and less rigid, clearly removing the persona she used in public. I guessed this was supposed to be a rare treat for me.

"It had nothing to do with blackmail. It had to do with letting him know that it was easy to find this in our opposition research. If it got into the wrong hands, it could have reflected poorly on him."

"Did my father know that you were the one who sent the photos?"

"He was aware because the return address was mine."

She didn't know how much she'd changed the trajectory of my life with her actions. She had no idea that my parents would have forced me to marry someone to keep all that quiet and how I defied their wishes by helping to expose my father. It wasn't something she needed to know.

Diana took a deep breath before continuing. "I wanted him to know that these were available so he could take the necessary steps to protect the reputation of his family. It would have been too easy to leak them myself and start some trouble, but that's not how I wanted to win an election. Then the information about him came out and..."

"Did you have anything to do with that?"

Diana shook her head vehemently. "Absolutely not. My

team didn't find out anything about that, so the information must have been buried pretty deep."

"Do you have any information on any other scandals I should probably know about?" I asked.

She sighed and shrugged before speaking. "There was nothing else major that we've come across, but I can't guarantee that there aren't more out there. We've done our due diligence, but you never know."

She rose from the table and stretched. "I don't want to stay in your hair for too much longer. I have another appointment I need to get to."

I watched as she gathered her purse and walked to the door. Just before she opened it and stepped across the threshold, I spoke again. "How did you know my father didn't already tell me you were the one who sent those photos?"

Diana turned to look back at me, her hand still on the door. "I can tell you're a very driven young woman, Bianca. That will get you far in life, trust me. But I assumed there was no way in hell you would have let me get away with sending those photos to your father without saying a word to me. I gave you some time in case he didn't talk to you about it right away, but I figured by now, enough was enough. Even if he hadn't informed you about the photos at all, I would have still admitted my involvement with them to you today."

With that, she walked away, leaving me in the conference room to ponder what the hell had just happened.

After a few minutes of replaying every second of what had just occurred over and over again in my head, I managed to get up from the desk, left the meeting room and headed to the elevator bank.

I checked my phone as I entered my apartment. Easton should be on his way back to my place soon.

But everything stopped when I looked down at the floor. I immediately backed out of my apartment and jogged back to the elevators. I put my phone to my ear and prayed that the call I needed to make would connect.

When it did, I almost yelled.

"Hello?"

"You need to get back here now."

22

UNKNOWN

I couldn't help but watch. I was sitting in a heavy armchair, its upholstery so black and sleek that it looked as if it belonged in a hip, minimalist bachelor's pad versus being a part of this lavish apartment building. I was pretending that I was reading the paper, engrossed in the current events going on around the world instead of what should be occurring sometime within the next hour.

I couldn't deny that I was enjoying the fact that I knew what was about to happen before anyone in this lobby did.

A couple of people studied Diana Caldwell when she walked in, speaking together in hushed voices as she walked by. It felt as if the whole room had stopped and all that could be heard over the soft murmurs was the sound of her heels clicking as she walked across the floor. I assumed residents recognized her from the campaign ads she'd been running. I knew that she'd raised plenty of money and had been giving Van Henson a run for his money even before the scandal broke.

Of course, I recognized her too, but I was excited about her arrival for an entirely different reason.

Diana walked up to the front desk. I assumed to ask for the woman of the hour. I watched as the attendant at the front desk told her that the person she was looking for wasn't answering their request and that maybe she should come back another time.

Diana looked around the lobby, slightly unsure of what she should do. I could understand that feeling because it reminded me of when I first started, having been thrown into this field. What I assumed she'd come here to do wasn't her forte. When she decided that she would stay and wait, I commended her because now she wasn't wasting both of our time. I settled back in the chair I was sitting in as anticipation grew within me. This upcoming meeting of two unlikely people was going to happen, and I had the best seat in the house to watch.

My attention shifted from what was going on in this lobby to what was occurring outside. A well-kept and polished black SUV pulled up to the front of the building and I couldn't help but grin because I recognized the vehicle easily.

Bianca.

She was finally here.

Since she had arrived, the next act of this scene was about to unfold.

The door of a black SUV opened, and I watched as she carefully stepped out of the vehicle.

I turned my gaze back to my newspaper for a moment to appear to be reading it once more. But I didn't read a single word. All of this was just to appear as if I was doing nothing more than sitting here waiting for someone, anyone, outside of the two women who were about to interact. As soon as I was certain that no one was paying me any mind, I turned my attention back to Bianca. She was about to get another big surprise. Her life seemed to be full of them these days.

Diana walked up to Bianca, and I watched as the sparks flew. I could feel the tension radiating off of both of them from here.

I wasn't close enough to hear what they were saying, but it was obviously contentious based on the emotions on their faces. Here they were, Bianca Henson and Diana Caldwell, two women on opposite sides of a political race, and I was the one who'd brought them together.

I watched as they both stopped talking for a second before the two women walked through the lobby and past me, going to where I knew there were workspaces for tenants of the building.

While I could try to follow the two women, there was no need. I already knew what their meeting would be about and why Diana was there. It was because of me, after all. I was the one who had made sure Diana's team would get those risqué photos of Bianca. Based on Diana's desire to work and perform with dignity, I thought it was a safe bet that she would give them to Van Henson versus leaking them herself, and I was right.

I folded up my newspaper before standing up and walking to the exit. While I was only a spectator, I'd held a puppeteer's control over the events that had just unfolded and ones I hadn't anticipated, like Van being willing to set up an arranged marriage for his daughter.

It was time to retreat because I'd already overstayed my welcome. This game was slowly coming to an end as I'd set out to do what I wanted to do, including leaving a small present in Bianca's apartment for her. With a final glance around the lobby, I walked to the glass doors and stepped into the cold, rainy weather.

After all, I had other places to be.

23

EASTON

I unlocked the door to my apartment and stepped across the threshold as I took in a deep breath. The familiar sight was relaxing in a way and always had a way of welcoming me back home. Nothing had been changed or disturbed since I'd left days ago. I shrugged off my coat and tossed it on the back of a chair in my living room before I headed for my bedroom.

I quickly pulled out some of the clothes that I would need to use at Bianca's. While Bianca had decided to wait to shower until she got home, I'd showered in my old bathroom and only needed to change out of some of the clothes I'd left at home. I quickly changed into a pair of jeans, a faded T-shirt, and a hoodie and repacked my bag that I kept in my car. I needed to call the laundry service I sometimes used to wash and dry my clothes.

As I was walking back into the living room with my bag, I debated grabbing a bottle of water before I left when my phone buzzed in my pocket, pulling me out of my thoughts.

The screen flashed Nash's name, and I answered it before it could buzz again.

"Hey, man, what's up?" I asked as I wondered why he was calling me instead of texting.

"Easton, I want you to check this out," Nash said, his tone urgent. "I've got some intel on Soren Grant that you need to see. But this is confidential information, so you didn't see a thing."

This hadn't been what I was expecting him to say, but I was happy, nonetheless. "Alright, I get it. Send it over," I said. If there was something about Soren that could help us get Iris back, I needed to know.

"You're going to need to access the secure network on your laptop. I'll guide you through it," Nash instructed.

"What are you talking about? I don't have access to any other network outside of the school's."

"Yes, you do. Let me help you through it."

"But—"

"We don't have time to waste."

He was right. I needed to focus on the information he'd gathered, not how I suddenly had access to this network I could have sworn wasn't on my computer a few weeks ago, but was definitely there now.

Nash walked me through the process of accessing the secured network, and I saw a list of files before me. "Which one do I need to view?"

"File 4-3-7-9. You won't believe the shit this guy can do, Easton. But before you look—"

"Holy shit," I said as I scanned the file before me. There wasn't much about Soren's personal biography in it, but specific details on some of his specialties were nothing to mess around with, to say the least. Nothing in his file alluded to why he would bother kidnapping Iris though.

"See what I mean?" Nash said with a dark laugh. "The guy can track anyone, anywhere."

"Fuck," I muttered as I adjusted my phone. "How is this even possible?"

"Your guess is as good as mine."

"And are we absolutely certain that he's not the one after Bianca?"

Nash didn't say a word for a moment. "I still don't think he would have enough time to do what Bianca's stalker has been doing and keep Iris. Also, based on what I know about said stalker, they don't seem to have Soren's... abilities."

I actually agreed with his assessment, but wanted to see if he had anyone else in mind. "But was there anyone else that might have a similar skill set?"

"None that I can think of," Nash replied. "But it's worth looking into. I'll see if there's anyone else with the same skill set."

As I was about to hang up with Nash, my phone began vibrating in my hand, alerting me to another call. When I pulled the phone away from my ear, it gave me the option to answer Bianca's call or send it to voice mail.

Having her call me when I was supposed to be leaving my apartment for hers in a few minutes told me something was wrong.

"Shit, Nash, I have to go. I'll talk to you later." I didn't bother telling him goodbye as I quickly switched over to answer Bianca's call. "Bianca, what's going on? Are you okay?"

"You need to get back here now," she said, her voice

shaking slightly. "Someone has been in my apartment. I'll be downstairs in the lobby waiting on you."

"Fuck," I muttered under my breath as my adrenaline kicked in. "Okay, just stay put. I'm on my way. I'll call you when I'm in the car."

"Please hurry," she pleaded before hanging up.

I grabbed my coat and bag and bolted out of my apartment like it was on fire. Hearing the fear in her voice made me throw my bag in the passenger seat and tear out of my parking lot.

I used my SUV's Bluetooth to call Bianca, just like I promised, and I swore I could hear my pulse racing in my ears. Thankfully, she put me out of my misery and answered on the second ring.

"Easton."

"I'm in the car right now and I should be there in about twenty minutes, depending on traffic."

"Thank goodness," she replied before going silent for a few moments. "Easton?"

"Yes?"

"I'm scared," she said softly.

My heart clenched at hearing her say those words, feeling helpless because there was nothing I could do to make it better until I arrived at her apartment. "Bianca, just stay calm until I get there, okay? We'll figure this out together."

Whoever had put this fear into her heart was going to pay, and I couldn't wait to find the fucker.

Thankfully, my apartment wasn't too far away from hers, and I'd barely pulled my vehicle into a parking spot before I'd turned it off and was sprinting toward her building.

When Bianca spotted me, she ran toward me and ran into

my arms. "Easton, thank fuck you're here," Bianca exclaimed.

We were attracting attention, but neither one of us cared. When she pulled away, her eyes were wide and frantic, and her chest was heaving as if she'd just run a marathon.

"You need to see this. Now."

"Okay, let's go," I said. The two of us took the elevator up to her apartment, but when she opened the door, I didn't immediately notice that anything was wrong. It wasn't until she stepped forward and bent down to pick up something that it all clicked into place.

"Look at this," she said, shoving the item in my face. I recognized it immediately, and I wasn't surprised that she had done the same. It was a coin with the Chevaliers emblem, and someone had left it in her apartment. It wasn't mine because it was something you received once you were placed in one of the three chambers of the Chevalier organization: Owl, Eagle, and Sparrow. That wouldn't happen until the beginning of next semester.

"Who the fuck was here?" I demanded, wanting an answer immediately. I clenched my fists so hard I could feel my nails digging into the palms of my hand.

"I have no idea," Bianca said, weighing the coin with her hand. "But now we definitely know that the person who is stalking me is a Chevalier."

"Well then, we know what our next stop is. Let's go."

I stormed out of Bianca's apartment, angrier than I'd ever been in my life. I didn't know exactly what was going on, but having it confirmed that the Chevaliers had sent someone after my girl was enough for me to want to make the world burn. The organization that I'd pledged to had just become enemy number one.

24

BIANCA

The coin in my hand with the Chevalier emblem on it sent a cold shiver down my spine.

I'd gotten cocky in a way. I'd thought because we didn't notice anything weird about my apartment when we got back from Italy, my stalker wouldn't bother trying to break in.

But now they had.

I'd only been gone overnight, giving my stalker less time to break into my apartment. But he'd done it, nonetheless.

"But why now?" My hands trembled as I stared at the coin in my hand as I sat in the passenger seat of Easton's SUV.

"Call Nash."

"Say what?" I said as I was jerked out of my thoughts.

"Call Nash. He needs to meet us at Chevalier Manor."

I placed the coin down in my lap and picked up my phone. I was a little bit klutzy when it came to finding Nash's number, but I managed to call him and put the call on speaker.

"Hello?"

"Hey. Easton is here with me too, by the way. Can you meet us at Chevalier Manor?" I asked, and I was proud that I was able to keep my voice steady.

"I'm already here. What's up? Are you okay?"

"Um. Are you alone?"

"No. Let me step outside."

I could feel my heart pounding in my chest as if it was going to burst out and leave my body. I waited patiently for Nash to tell me that he'd ventured outside, and it felt like a lifetime had passed.

"I'm alone. What happened?"

I took in a deep breath to try to calm myself so that I could get the story I needed to tell out. "I unlocked my apartment door, and as I was about to walk in, I found a gold coin with the Chevalier emblem on it."

Nash didn't respond, and I wasn't surprised. He was probably running through every scenario about how that coin had ended up in my apartment. "How long will it take you guys to get here?"

This time, Easton spoke up. "We are about ten minutes away."

With how fast he was going, I wouldn't be surprised if we got there in half the time.

Rain hit the windshield and I was a little concerned that we might crash, given the speed we were traveling and the weather. The wipers swished back and forth in a rhythm that could have been therapeutic at any other time.

It took a few minutes, but the trees seemed to part as if they were giving us a path to Chevalier Manor. The quiet and eerie atmosphere was enough for me to stay on edge even though it was daylight.

When we were a couple of minutes away, I saw the old mansion, and it gave me the same vibes that Westwick University tended to give me: the fucking creeps.

Easton pulled to a stop in a parking spot and turned to look at me. "You know, it would be safer for you to stay out here in this car with everything locked down."

"But you know there is no way I would willingly stay here. We don't even know if whoever is doing it is at Chevalier Manor right now."

"Which is why I didn't tell you that you were staying here and that was final."

"Even if you did, I wouldn't listen. You can tell me what to do in bed, but I draw the line at you trying to boss me around when we're out of it."

"It's not bossing you around if I'm keeping you safe."

I sighed. "Nash is going to be there too. Between the two of you, I'll be fine."

"Then let's go."

We got out of the car and once we were near the hood, Easton grabbed my hand, and we hurried toward the entrance because of the rain. We didn't say a word as we walked up to the large, black front door; it opened, revealing Nash standing there with a serious expression on his face.

The firm grip of Easton's hand wrapped around mine helped calm me slightly as I stared back at my brother. Nash's gaze shifted from me and focused on Easton, probably questioning why the hell he'd bring me here if something was going to happen, but I hadn't given Easton much of a choice either. Plus, I didn't want to be alone if the stalker was here.

I dug into my coat pocket, grabbed what I wanted, and stuck my hand out so Nash could take it.

The coin with the Chevalier emblem on it. Nash studied it for a moment before he pocketed it and turned to let us into the building.

I knew deep down that he was at a crossroads with the organization he was supposed to lead on this campus, especially with them having no issue with sending one of their own after us.

The weather outside did nothing to help the darkness that seemed to fill Chevalier Manor. Easton's eyes scanned the foyer of the building as Nash closed the door behind us.

"Stay close," Easton whispered before his eyes went back to darting around the room. There wasn't any doubt that I would because I didn't know what any of the people in this house were capable of.

Entering the mysterious place did nothing but fuel the tension that had been suffocating me since I'd arrived at my apartment earlier today. While I was hopeful that all of this would end today, I was afraid of what we might find.

My anxiety about all of this had me wanting to find the nearest bottle of alcohol and take a swig, but I couldn't.

"What do we do now?" I asked. I didn't know if, somehow, telepathically, Easton and Nash had thought of a way to handle this, but I was completely clueless.

Nash spoke up. "Why don't you and Easton look around upstairs and I'll focus on downstairs, and we'll meet up here in fifteen minutes?"

"What if there's nothing here?" I asked because we didn't even know what we were looking for.

Nash held up the coin. "This was a hint that we needed to look around here. I know it."

"So, this could potentially be a fucked-up wild-goose chase," I replied.

"That's one way to put it," Easton chimed in.

"It won't be. It should be easy enough to look around because this place should be just about empty, with everyone being home for winter break. Let's get this done, and if you find anything, call me."

My brother walked away, leaving Easton and me alone to go and do our own investigation. I turned to Easton, and he held out his hand once more and together we ascended the stairs, listening intently to see if we heard anything.

But the only thing we could hear was the light sounds of our breathing as we stilled just outside the hallway.

Easton and I slowly made our way down a long hallway filled with doors. We tried the doorknobs to see if any of them were unlocked. We didn't want to invade anyone's privacy, but if one just so happened to be unlocked, we checked to see if anyone was in there.

Room after room that we could access was empty, which was what we'd expected.

When we tried one of the last remaining doors, Easton walked in first and turned on the light.

I gasped as I took in the sight before me.

There was someone there. Sitting in one of the chairs that were standard in every dorm room on Brentson's campus.

And I recognized him.

Words seemed to fail me as I stared at the man in front of me, all the while trying to piece together what was going on.

"Landon? What the hell are you doing here?"

He stood up slowly, his gaze focused on me. "I'm here because I'm the reason why you're here."

As realization about what his words meant hit me, a surge of nausea shot through my body. Easton took a step forward and gently pushed me behind him. "You've been stalking Bianca?"

Before Landon could confirm or deny Easton's accusation, Easton let go of my hand and lunged forward to grab Landon. I ran toward the door because there was no way I was going to be able to get between the two of them and stop what was about to happen. Just as I was about to scream, Nash rushed into the room but came to a stop at seeing Easton holding Landon up against a wall.

"You son of a bitch," Easton spat, his hands wrapped around Landon's throat, making it hard for him to talk. "How fucking dare you?"

Landon's choked laughter filled the room, an echo that would haunt me for years, if not forever. There was something in his eyes, a spark of defiance despite the position he was in, that made my skin crawl. But still, he didn't confirm or deny that he was indeed the one who was stalking me.

But Easton didn't care. When I heard the slamming of Easton's fist connecting with Landon's face, I covered my face in horror. I was convinced that the only way Landon was still upright was because of the hold Easton had on his neck.

Nash glanced back at me before he turned back to Landon. "What the fuck are you doing? Why are you coming forward now?"

"Because," Landon started, and I assumed Easton loosened the grip on his neck to give him a chance to speak, "my mission is complete."

I dropped my hands from my face in shock. Wait a minute. Was Landon admitting to stalking me because the higher-ups in the Chevalier world had wanted him to? *What the fuck? I swear, at this point, I still have more questions than answers.*

Easton's voice broke through my thoughts, and I watched as he turned to look at Nash. "How much trouble would I get in for killing someone who is also a member of the Chevaliers? Because I'm willing to risk it all."

And that was when the stakes changed.

25

EASTON

With my fist clenched and my heart pounding, I stood in the same building where I professed that I would dedicate my life to serving the Chevaliers. And where one of them had betrayed me.

What occurred in the basement of this place replayed in my mind as I tried to take deep breaths. My knuckles ached with the desire to slam into Landon's smug face. To wipe that shit-eating grin off his lips and make him pay for what he'd done, once and for all.

Landon tried to roll his shoulders back while I held him up against the wall. Fucker wasn't even worried.

It was interesting how much confidence he had for someone who was just minutes away from death.

I glared at the man in front of me before turning to Nash. "How much trouble would I get in for killing someone who is also a member of the Chevaliers? Because I'm willing to risk it all."

And I meant every word.

The next moment, everything went to shit. Landon took

advantage of my momentary lapse of attention and lunged at me. I swung first, but he dodged my hand and his fist landed on my jaw. Pain exploded through my skull. I stumbled back, vision blurring, but I refused to give up.

Fists were flying in every direction as Nash joined in on the fight. It was obvious that Landon was a trained fighter because he was able to dodge some hits and land a few of his own, even though he was up against two people.

I could smell the metallic scent of fresh blood as it filled the air as we fought each other, and it only enraged me further.

I hated that Bianca was witnessing it, but I couldn't get myself to stop.

Landon pushed me off him briefly, sending me backward slightly before I caught myself. "Is that all you got?" he exclaimed as his eyes darted between Nash and me.

It wasn't. Not by a long shot.

Deep within me, a roar started, making its way up from my gut, and I charged at him once more. This time, my fist found its mark.

Landon's head snapped to the side, blood flying from his mouth. It was obvious to me that he hadn't been expecting the hit as he spat the blood out before proceeding to swing at me wildly.

I ducked and slammed my knee into his stomach. Landon proceeded to double over with a grunt. Before I could do anything else, Nash kicked him in the chest, and then I grabbed him by the collar of his shirt and pulled him upright.

"Do you have any last words?"

Before Landon could respond, a loud yell filled the air. "Enough!"

Everyone froze at the sound of the voice. Parker Townsend, chairman of every chapter of the Chevaliers in New York State, walked the room.

"Cut it the fuck out." Parker's glare shifted from me to Nash and then to Landon. "I will not tolerate this kind of behavior."

"Not until this fucker is dead," I called out.

"Watch your tone with me, Beaumont."

Anger still pulsated through me. "This asshole was stalking her, and I won't let him get away with it."

"As the new chairman of the Chevaliers on this campus, I won't tolerate any insubordination, especially when it is against my family."

Parker's eyes drilled down to look at Nash. "He's not disobeying any rules."

I took a step toward Parker because to hell with toeing the line. "The hell he isn't."

This time, Parker glared at me. "He's not disobeying anyone because I asked him to keep an eye on her."

Silence filled the room as Parker's words hung in the air. Stunned didn't even begin to describe how I, and I was sure Nash and Bianca, felt. The surprises continued to hit us with no sign of slowing down.

It was then I realized how much my jaw ached and saw the bloodstains on my knuckles, but none of that compared to the thoughts crashing inside me like I was on the world's biggest roller coaster.

Hell, it was a roller coaster of emotions, quite frankly.

Anger. Frustration. Helplessness.

Thankfully, Nash had enough sense to speak up. "Why was he keeping tabs on her?"

Parker's attention turned to Bianca, who was still standing near the door. She looked ready to bolt at any moment, and I didn't blame her. When Parker didn't say a word immediately, I made my way toward her and pulled her into my arms to give her the support she needed. And I didn't care what anyone in this room had to say about it.

"Why was he watching her, Parker?" The words carried all the heat I felt about the turn of events. I didn't care about respecting the man in front of me, who could probably order that I be killed on the spot. I wouldn't be surprised if he tried to do it himself, for that matter. None of that mattered though. I was going to get answers, one way or another. The fact that even Nash was kept in the dark about this was astounding.

"I ordered Landon to do this because we needed to see how involved she was with a matter pertaining to the safety and security of the Chevaliers because of someone she is associated with. Today we deemed that this matter was closed, so Landon will no longer be watching Bianca."

"Chairman, that's not good enough," I said without thinking about it too much. There was no way he was being serious. The need to quench my desire to know what was going on was not satisfied with his answer.

Parker took a step toward Bianca and me, increasing the tension in the room. He met my anger with an icy calm. "It's going to have to be good enough for you, Beaumont."

The tone of his voice was almost daring me to ask more questions after he'd obviously dismissed my line of questioning.

Why? What was the point of being vague now?

This time, Nash moved to stand next to me while Landon

slowly made his way to stand next to Parker. It felt as if there was a line drawn in the sand and this group was standing on opposite sides of it.

"Does this have anything to do with Iris's disappearance?"

The whole room was shocked when Bianca spoke up, and everyone but Parker turned to stare at her. His gaze had never left her.

"Landon, head down to my car. It's time to leave."

His non-answer was the answer we needed. Iris's disappearance had everything to do with Landon stalking Bianca. And all of that had something to do with protecting the Chevaliers.

Landon walked around us, staring as he left. The urge to throw another punch was there, but I let him walk by.

Parker made a move to walk toward the door, but just before he left, he said, "Landon's mission is done. Bianca, you don't have to worry about him anymore."

"But where is Iris? Is she okay?" Bianca's questions fell on deaf ears because Parker just walked by us and left the room.

I grabbed Bianca's hands and asked, "Are you okay?"

She nodded. "I'm fine."

I pulled her into my arms, enjoying the feel of her in them again. "I'm sorry you had to see all of that."

"It's okay, but what are we going to do?" Her voice was muffled against my chest. "Parker's protecting Landon for some reason, and Iris is somehow caught up in all of this. The most I'd heard about her connection to the Chevaliers was about the party she attended that they'd held on Westwick's campus."

"We have to handle this ourselves." I glanced over at Nash, who was looking at both of us.

Our gazes met, and a silent understanding passed between us. We were willing to follow Parker's direction, but he didn't say anything about not trying to find Iris. At least now, according to him, Bianca would no longer be bothered. But how much did we fully trust him in regard to that?

No matter what the status of everything was, I needed to get Bianca out of there.

"We're leaving," I announced. I was surprised at how steady my voice sounded because I was still seething.

Bianca looked down at my bruised knuckles before she looked back up at me. "Okay."

Together, Nash, Bianca, and I walked downstairs and out the front door of Chevalier Manor.

The rain had stopped, as though it, too, had realized what had just happened inside this building. The crisp, cold air tried to cool me down, but I wasn't sure how much it actually helped.

Bianca and I walked to my SUV and got inside. I could hear the deep breath that Bianca just let loose as we both stared back at Chevalier Manor.

She was also the first to break our silence. "What the hell just happened in there?"

We looked at one another as we both tried to process the magnitude of what had just occurred. What Parker did and didn't reveal had answered several questions we'd had, but it was also a bomb he'd dropped on us without any warning.

"I'm not sure," I confessed, running a hand through my hair in frustration. It was difficult to put my emotions into words as my brain was still in fight mode.

We watched Nash lock the front door and then he walked over to us. He looked pretty bad after the fight we'd gotten into with Landon, and I assumed I looked similarly. I rolled down Bianca's window so that we could talk.

"You're going to take her home?"

"Yes, that is the plan. I think we all need to relax; if I do say so myself."

"Take care of yourself, Nash," Bianca said. It was easy to hear the concern she had for her brother in her voice.

"I will. I'm sure Raven will force me to sit down somewhere once she finds out what happened."

"Good. We'll talk later. I love you, bro."

Nash gave a small smile. "And I love you too."

Nash walked away from my vehicle, and as he made his way to his car, I pulled out of the parking spot and sped down the road. As the distance between us and Chevalier Manor increased, I finally slowed, turning to glance at Bianca before shifting my attention back to the road.

"Are you sure you're okay?"

"I'm fine," Bianca said. I could hear the slight annoyance in her voice because I was asking her again, but I didn't care. I needed to know that she was okay. "Are you okay?"

"I'm sure my hand and face are telling a different story, but I am. And I would do it again in a heartbeat. I love you, Bianca."

"And I love you."

26

BIANCA

The simple words we shared with one another were enough to cause something in me to break. Tears welled in my eyes, blurring my vision as I tried to maintain my composure.

"It's partially over, princess," he whispered as he grabbed my hand. He brought it up to his lips and placed a small kiss on the back of it. "We just need to find Iris now."

Through my tear-streaked vision, I nodded, pulling away to meet his gaze. "I know, but I'm so worried about her. Worried that Parker was lying."

I wiped my eyes as I looked at him and noticed that a muscle jumped in his jaw. He couldn't help but think Parker was full of shit too. I stared at him for ten seconds until he spoke. "I don't think he's lying."

"Why is that?"

"Because he hasn't lied throughout any of this. Sure, he's avoided answering questions, but he hasn't outright said something and then we've discovered the opposite. So, I do think Landon will no longer be following you. Now, while I'm still not letting you out of my sight for a while, I do think he was being truthful about that."

I turned away from Easton to look out the window as we drove through downtown Brentson. To me, there wasn't anything like the shops and scenery here.

It was then I realized I felt safe. It was the first time in a long time that I could honestly say that I felt this way.

Even though I didn't live too far from campus, Easton drove for what felt like forever until we finally reached my building. He parked the car and turned off the engine before facing me. "We should talk to your building security about how easy it was for someone to access your apartment."

"Can we do that tomorrow? After everything today, I'm just ready to finally take the hot shower I wanted to take hours ago."

"That sounds like a good plan," Easton replied.

He opened his door and stepped out before walking around to open my door. I waited as Easton walked around to the back seat and pulled a duffel bag out of the vehicle. He held out his hand for me to grab and together, we walked into my apartment building. Flashes of my meeting with Diana Caldwell crossed my mind as we walked over to the elevator bank. Thankfully, the elevator was already there, and within a couple of minutes, we were walking into my apartment.

"I don't think I've ever been as happy to be here as I am right now," I said, tossing my keys onto the counter.

Easton didn't answer but sent me a tired smile.

"Hey, let me take a look at where you got hurt." My concern for him took over, and I motioned for him to sit on my couch by the window. As he lowered himself, I followed suit to get a closer look at his injuries. His face was a bit of a mess—swollen, bruised, and there was a cut on his forehead. His clothes were wrinkled too, and I wondered if he had any bruises on his chest.

I grabbed ice from the kitchen before I headed to the bathroom to gather supplies. Moments later, I returned with a bowl of warm water, some antiseptic, bandages, and a towel.

"Alright, let's get you cleaned up." I handed him the ice to put on his jaw. I dipped the cloth into the water and gently dabbed at the cut on his forehead. Easton winced but didn't pull away. At least he wasn't a shitty patient.

"Thanks, Bianca," Easton murmured, his eyes meeting mine. "I appreciate this."

"Of course." I took a deep breath and said, "You've got my back, and I've got yours. That's how love works, right?"

"Right." He smiled.

I couldn't help the warmth that spread through my chest, even as I continued to clean and take care of his wounds.

"Almost done," I promised as I finished wiping the now-dried blood off his knuckles. "Relax. Doctor's orders," I said with a wink.

"Got it," Easton said as he smiled again. He slowly leaned back on the couch, and I grabbed my throw blanket and laid it on top of him.

"Hey, do you need anything else?" I asked as I stood up and prepared to throw out the garbage that had accumulated as a result of my doctoring Easton. "I'm going to take a quick shower and wanted to give you whatever you needed before I left you for a few minutes."

"I'll take some water, aspirin, and the remote."

"That's easy." I grabbed the remote and handed it to him. I threw out the trash and put the things I'd taken out away before grabbing a glass of water and aspirin for Easton.

"Thank you," he said just as I bent down to give him a kiss on the lips before I walked away.

Closing the bathroom door behind me, I turned on the shower and waited for the water to heat up. I stripped my clothes from my body and sighed. I couldn't help but stare at myself, my unmarked skin. Easton and Nash had put their bodies on the line to show their displeasure in Landon, and I'd made it out without a scratch on mine.

As steam began to fill up the room, I took my hair out of its ponytail and moved to step under the spray. The hot water spilled over me, and I watched it cascade down my body before circling the drain. It felt like a thousand tiny needles pricking my skin, but instead of feeling pain, I felt alive. More than I had in a long time.

I leaned my head against the tiled wall, enjoying the way the water helped soothe my soul and allowed me to escape from the chaos that had wanted to claim my life.

The scent of citrus and lavender filled my nostrils as I washed my hair and lathered my body up with soap. I scrubbed the day's events from my skin and hair, but I couldn't scrub them from my mind. Like a movie, the scene at Chevalier Manor played over and over again. Landon being there was a shock because I didn't even know he was a Chevalier. Easton's eyes blazing with fury as he attacked Landon. Nash showing up just in time to join in on the fight.

My hands paused on my skin, the soapy suds running down an aimless path toward my feet as I remembered my reaction to Parker. I recalled the indifference in his voice as he'd revealed the fact that he ordered Landon to stalk me. The words echoed in my mind, a shitty mantra that described what had been my reality for weeks.

Finishing up, I rinsed my body before I turned off the water. As I stepped out of the shower, I grabbed a fluffy towel and wrapped it around myself. It took me a moment to gather another one and toss my hair into it. The plush fabric clung to my damp skin and hair and helped soak up moisture as I moved to the bathroom counter.

I took my time drying my body and putting lotion on my skin as I waited for the steam on the mirror to fade. Once I was finished and had thrown on a fancy robe, the mirror was clear enough for me to see myself. I grabbed my hairbrush and began to work through the tangles in my wet hair, appreciating the feeling of the bristles against my scalp. It was a mini head massage, and I needed one desperately after today's events.

I closed my eyes temporarily, enjoying the way I was treating myself to a few moments of self-care. When I opened my eyes, I almost jumped out of my skin. Easton was standing in the doorway, leaning against the frame. Our eyes met through the mirror I was standing in front of. He must have heard the water shut off and decided to come check on me.

We didn't say a word, simply held each other's gaze as we communicated our thoughts and feelings to one another without uttering a sound.

Easton pushed away from the doorframe and made his way over to me. His eyes never left mine in the mirror as he closed the distance between us. His stride was powerful and made me wonder what he wanted.

In one fluid motion, Easton wrapped his arms around my

waist, pulling me close to him. The brush fell out of my hand and clattered on the floor, but neither one of us moved to pick it up.

And then his lips met mine.

27

BIANCA

I t didn't take me long to realize that our kiss was full of raw emotion, given everything we'd been through. The kiss was nothing short of electrifying, sending sparks through every nerve in my body. My hands got tangled in his hair, and I knew I was grasping his strands as if I was holding on for dear life.

As we broke apart, panting for air, Easton whispered, "I need you."

His needing me instead of wanting me sent a shiver down my spine. "But you're hurt."

"I'm fine."

I couldn't help but let out a sarcastic chuckle. "You're far from fine."

"Baby, there is nothing wrong with my dick. I guarantee you I won't hear a single complaint coming from those pretty lips."

I knew he would make good on his promise. "Take me to bed," I murmured.

"That's what I always like to hear."

Easton placed his hands on the sides of my cheeks and kissed me once more. He started to walk toward me, crowding me and forcing me to back up and enter my bedroom.

His hands found the belt of my robe, and without hesitating, he ripped it open, causing it to land on my carpeted floor with a soft thud. He undressed himself, keeping in mind his injuries, and I was able to see a couple of additional areas that were starting to bruise.

None of that mattered, however.

I walked up to him and gently ran my hand down his chest and circled around the bruises I could see. I then leaned forward and placed a soft kiss on each one of them.

When I looked up into his eyes, I gasped at the emotion I saw in them, but it only lasted for a flash of a second.

Easton crowded me once more, forcing me to walk backward until the back of my legs hit my bed.

"I want you to sit on my face."

I was only too happy to comply.

He lay down on my bed and got comfortable before I climbed up on him.

As I made a move to sit up, my breasts ended up in Easton's face, and he made sure to take full advantage of the angle. He licked and lightly bit my nipples, forcing me to close my eyes as I took in the sensations he was sending through my body.

When he finally let me go, I was able to straddle his face, and he began licking and sucking my pussy. If I thought my senses were in overdrive from the attention he'd given my breasts, I was wrong because I could have sworn now he was working pure magic, which seemed to be shooting throughout my whole body.

All I could hear was the sound of my panting as his hands grasped my thighs tightly while his tongue played with my clit. I moaned as one of his hands left my thighs and made its way up to my breast, where he went back to playing with my nipple. He knew exactly what would make me moan with pleasure, and each time I did, he hummed in satisfaction.

And then I had an idea.

I tapped Easton's hands on my body, letting him know that I wanted him to stop. When he loosened his grip on me, I moved my body, so I wasn't straddling him, then turned around, putting my legs back around his body.

It took a second for him to realize what I was doing.

"Oh fuck, baby."

"Mmhmm," I said as I lay down on him softly so that I was able to grab his cock. "I'll be gentle."

"Maybe I don't want you to be."

"That can be arranged as well."

I didn't wait for him to say another word before I stuck his dick in my mouth.

I swear I could feel his groan cause a small vibration between my thighs. But even as he was feeling his own pleasure, he didn't stop sucking my clit and driving me insane.

I stopped sucking his dick for a moment to take a deep breath in an effort to relax my throat. Then I stuck his cock back in my mouth and took more of him in, and all the while, he continued the assault on my pussy.

I could feel myself growing closer to my climax and it made it harder to focus on what I was doing to Easton. That was until Easton's voice cut through the haze I was in.

"Stop sucking me off, Bianca."

His dick popped out of my mouth due to my confusion. "Why?"

"Because I want you to sink down on my cock, princess."

After everything he'd done for me, who was I to deny him when it would send us both over the edge?

I shifted my body and turned so that we were looking at each other once more. I made sure to straddle him again, this time his lower body instead of his face. Once our bodies were aligned, I sank down on him, making sure to be careful not to touch any of the areas where I could see bruising.

When his cock was fully seated in me, I threw my head back and groaned, happy that we'd finally made it to this point.

"Fuck, Bianca," he said as his hands gripped my hips. "You feel so damn good."

That was all the encouragement I needed to start moving. This position allowed me to take control of the pace. I started off slow and steady to ensure that he would be okay because of the pain he must have been feeling. As I moved, his eyes locked onto mine, and I swallowed hard as I saw all the love that there was for me in them.

Soon enough, I found my own rhythm, and I started increasing the intensity of my movements. His fingernails started digging into my hips as he helped guide me.

I could feel my body shaking the closer I grew to my own release, and that was when I felt him thrust up into me, meeting the movements I made perfectly.

I watched him, seeing so many emotions cross his face before he closed his eyes and let out a low groan. That was all

I needed to see to conclude that he was closing in on his own release as well.

I bit the corner of my lip as his eyes opened once more, meeting mine. I could see the raw need in them, and it was time for us to give into the pleasure we both wanted to succumb to.

I moved to quicken our rhythm, leaning backward slightly to change the angle that we were fucking. Without missing a beat, Easton matched my energy as it felt as if our bodies were becoming one.

"Easton, I—" Words failed me as the sensations that coursed through me threatened to consume me whole.

"Come for me, princess," he urged and that was all it took.

The sexual tension in the air snapped, and I was swept up in a wave of ecstasy as I sailed off into orgasmic bliss, and Easton followed right behind me.

"Holy fuck," Easton said, in between trying to catch his breath. "That was... indescribable."

I slowly leaned forward and lay on his chest, enjoying the feeling of him still in me. "Are you okay?" I asked, worried that he might have gotten hurt while we were having fun.

"Never been better," he said, putting his arms around me and giving me a huge hug. I was still trying to not put too much weight on him.

"Good," I whispered against his chest, feeling the weight of everything we'd been through slowly start to slip away.

With our bodies tangled together and sweat cooling on our skin, I couldn't help but feel a sense of peace. It made sense for us to get up and clean ourselves off, but for right now, it felt nice to just be in his arms. The chaos from Chevalier Manor felt like a distant memory even though it had only been about an hour ago and the physical reminders still lingered.

"Princess," Easton whispered, the sound only slightly louder than his beating heart. "Why don't we watch something on television and just veg out?"

That was something I could get behind. "Sounds perfect, but after we get cleaned up."

We both finally moved to disentangle ourselves from one another, and we headed to the bathroom to clean ourselves. We then walked back into my bedroom, both of us naked as the day we were born, and climbed back into bed. I reached over to grab the television remote and handed it to Easton for him to find something for us to watch. I was pretty sure I was going to fall asleep anyway, so there wasn't a point in me looking for something to watch.

"Any preference?" Easton asked as he scrolled through the endless list of movies and shows.

I shrugged. "Feel free to surprise me."

He selected an action movie, which was fine by me. We spent the rest of our afternoon wrapped up in each other's arms, dozing on and off as the movie played in the background.

28

BIANCA

I was curled up in the corner of my couch in my apartment, my gaze stuck on my window as light snow fell from the sky. It set an eerie tone for the day ahead. I was thankful to be able to sit underneath this cozy blanket in my warm apartment with the cold, dreary weather outside. But what I was doing was procrastinating about the call I needed to make.

I picked up the sleek phone that Tristan had given me ahead of my trip to Italy from the coffee table. My fingers traced the cool, smooth surface as I found his number and waited for the phone to connect our call.

I heard it ring a few times before Tristan picked up. "Hello, Bianca," he said. His voice immediately made me think of how we'd almost gotten engaged until I decided to take charge. "What can I do for you?"

"Hey," I replied. "I wanted to thank you for everything."

"Thank me?"

"Yes. The private plane to Naples, the money for my expenses, this phone that helped me vanish essentially and for telling Easton where I was." Each instance brought a flush of warm memories, each more cherished than the last.

"It was the least I could do. Did you enjoy the trip?"

"Yes, it was incredible. I think it is something that I won't ever forget. Oh, and I will return the phone to you when I'm back in New York City. And I can send you back the rest of the money I didn't spend."

Tristan waited a beat before he responded. "Don't worry about the money. I'm not missing it. No rush on the phone either. You can take your time."

"I appreciate it," I said just before I cleared my throat. "I don't want to take up too much more of your time, but before I let you go, I have a question I want to ask you."

It was something that had been circling the back of my mind since the news about my father broke and I should take this as an opportunity to ask it.

"What is it?"

"Who sent the video of my father with the escort to you?"

There was a long pause on the other end, and it made me wonder if I should have asked the question at all. When Tristan finally replied, his voice was serious. "It was submitted anonymously, Bianca. We don't know who sent the video in. Even if I did know, I wouldn't be able to tell you because we keep our sources to ourselves."

A chill ran down my spine at his words and I suddenly became colder than what any winter gust could bring. I swallowed hard. The weight of the situation was suddenly very real.

"Okay," was all I could say. "Thank you once again, Tristan."

The call ended, leaving me alone with my thoughts, but

that was only for a moment because the knock on my door jerked me out of my thoughts. I hadn't been expecting anyone with Easton spending time with his parents today, so who could it be?

A flash of Landon standing on the other side of the door flitted through my mind as I walked to the front door. But once I took a second to look out of the peephole, I realized that I was completely wrong, and it made sense why the front desk had let this person up without alerting me.

It was my mom. And the guilt and sadness in her eyes were unmistakable.

I wasn't prepared for this.

With a deep breath, I yanked the door open and looked at the person standing on the other side. Before I could form a word, she took a step forward and wrapped her arms around me. It was something unexpected, and it knocked the air out of my lungs without squeezing me hard.

I could feel her body trembling against mine and I couldn't help but wonder what was wrong. What had brought her here?

"I'm so sorry, Bianca," she said in between sobbing into my shoulder. "I'm so sorry for everything I've done...for all the pain I've caused you."

"Mom..." I whispered as my own eyes started to sting. I tried to hold back tears. A part of me wanted to push her away, to tell her it was too late for her to apologize, but another part craved this connection we once had. Before my father entered politics. Before it changed our entire world. My hands hovered over her back, unsure of whether I wanted to reciprocate the hug or not.

"What are you doing here?" I finally said as I tried to

swallow the emotion in my voice. At the sound of my question, she pulled back slightly, her tear-streaked face searching mine for any sign of forgiveness.

Before she could talk, I took a step back, allowing her to enter my apartment so that this wouldn't happen in the doorway. I didn't need my neighbors to hear every part of the conversation I was probably going to have with my mother.

"I needed to see you," she said, sniffling as she tried to calm herself down. "I waited to come over to give you some time away from your father and me. I want to do better and be there for you like I should have been for all of these years." Her voice cracked and she swiped at her eyes with the back of her hand.

"Was what Dad did to me the last time we saw each other a turning point?"

Mom seemed shocked by my question. "No. The news of his affairs was. Not having you there when the news broke was."

"I didn't even realize you knew I was missing."

Mom's eyes opened wide in shock. "Of course I did. I took Tristan's explanation as a fact, but I did want to know where you were. I'm glad you weren't here to see everything that happened. I wish you hadn't been there to see me throw that vase at your father."

I couldn't tell if her cheeks were turning red because she was embarrassed or from the tears she was crying.

The tears in my mother's eyes sparked something deep within me, and I couldn't help but feel the walls I'd built around my mind and heart start to crumble. Hell, they started to crumble when I saw how upset my mother was the evening before the fateful night that my father acted as if he was going to lunge at me. Tentatively, I wrapped my arms around her, allowing myself to fully embrace her.

"I know I don't deserve your forgiveness, Bianca, but I'll work hard to show you that I want to be in your life. I will do anything for us to start the process of rebuilding the relationship we once had."

The weight of her words sank in, almost crushing me as I replayed them over and over. Could I really find it in myself to fully forgive her? It was a terrifying thought, if I was being honest, but a small part of me yearned to feel the love of my mother again that wasn't tied to anything to do with politics.

As I stood with my mother just arm's length away from me, I felt something inside me shift. All the pain and betrayal didn't disappear in an instant, but the heavy weight on my chest seemed to lift ever so slightly. It felt nice not to feel the burden of all of this pain anymore.

"Okay, Mom," I said softly, my eyes locked with hers. "Let's give this a shot. I want to try to rebuild our relationship."

Mom fell into my arms again and cried once more.

29

BIANCA

A FEW DAYS LATER

The deep breathing exercises I'd been performing to distract myself weren't working. The SUV slowed down before it came to a stop. The peaceful ambience in the vehicle didn't do a thing to stop my heart from hammering in my chest. Even with Easton here, sitting in the driver's seat, it wasn't doing anything to calm me down.

Today could be it. It could fix a lot of things. I'd been wanting to do this for a long time, but the thought of what I might find, or my being too late, might make me throw up.

The gothic mansion stood before us, nestled among towering trees on a hill. It felt as if it was surrounded by darkness, even though it was the middle of the afternoon. Its outer appearance was weathered and aged by time and there were so many windows that I wouldn't even bother trying to count all of them because I knew I would fail. Two crumbling stone statues guarded the entrance to the home, and the state of them was freaking me the fuck out.

Or maybe it was what I might find on the other side of the front door that was making me panic.

It looked the same as I remembered it as a kid and when I stopped by a few weeks ago. I wasn't surprised that my childhood friends and I thought it was haunted. Hell, maybe it was.

Easton killed the engine, and we were surrounded by silence, which was thick and suffocating. It spread around us like a dense fog, and I wouldn't have been surprised if a fog had drifted down from the mansion we were parked in front of.

He turned to me, his green eyes shifting between me and the house we were in front of. "Are you ready?"

"Yes, I am."

But that was a lie.

Shit. What had I gotten us into?

I swallowed hard; my mouth suddenly as dry as a desert. Everything in me screamed to tell Easton to start the engine and get us the hell out of here. However, I couldn't back down now.

Easton squeezed my hand before he opened his door. I followed his lead and stepped out of the vehicle.

I pulled my coat tighter around me as I felt the crunch of gravel under my boots and listened to the sharp sound of my steps breaking the silence. The sound penetrated, seeming to echo around us and forced me to bite back a scream due to it and the fear and anticipation for what was about to happen.

By the time we walked up the crumbling steps to the front door, I was a hot, nervous mess. While I knew Easton wouldn't let anything happen to me, I still couldn't stop my nerves from spinning.

I raised my fist and pounded on the dark, heavy oak door. As we waited for someone to respond, Easton moved so that I was slightly behind him. The door creaked open slowly and a man loomed in the doorway, tall and gaunt, clad in an all-black suit. His eyes were pale, and his face was very angular.

For some reason, I'd been expecting Soren Grant to answer his own door, but I was completely wrong. And I wasn't sure if I'd wished he had.

There was nothing good about any of this. I felt it deep down in my bones. But I remained focused on the goal that brought us here.

I stood up taller, even though I wanted to fold like a house of cards and asked, "Where is Iris Bennington?"

The man's pale eyes flicked between us, and I could see the cold and calculating nature of them. If I didn't already have a sense of unease about this situation, I definitely would have now.

Then he did the last thing I expected him to do. He smiled, thin and sharp like a knife's edge, but he said nothing at all.

I glanced at Easton, but there was no expression on his handsome face. His jaw was set in a hard line.

"Where is Iris?" I said again, struggling to keep my voice even.

The man tilted his head as his gaze narrowed. "And who are you?"

My breath caught in my throat. My emotions jumped between dread and hope. I couldn't decide which. But I refused to show weakness. I kept my chin high and glared at the man standing there, barring the threshold. "Take me to her. Now."

"Bianca—" Easton's warning was cut off by the man stepping aside with a graceful sweep of his arm.

"Please, come in," the man said.

Every instinct screamed not to cross over the threshold. But we couldn't turn back now.

I looked at Easton to see what he was thinking. He gave a slight nod, jaw clenched, and he put his hand on my lower back as we stepped into the creepy house together.

The heavy door shut behind us, the sound a resounding boom that echoed around the room. My heart pounded as my eyes adjusted to the dim light within.

This was a mistake.

But it was too late.

EPILOGUE

BIANCA

Two and a Half Years Later

Outside was abuzz with excitement and chatter as I walked down the aisle in my cap and gown. Four years of hard work that included all-nighters at the library, lots of drinks during my freshmen and sophomore year, and an existential crisis or two finally paid off. I was ready to walk across that stage and move on to the next stage of my life.

Well, that's how I felt right then. Yesterday, I couldn't help but cry at the fact that I was graduating.

As I looked into the sea of faces, my gaze instinctively sought out the familiar ones that belonged to my family. First, my eyes landed on my mother. She was dabbing at her eyes with a wadded-up tissue, while my father remained stoic on the other side of her. It had taken some time, but they were in the process of getting divorced because my mom realized there was no way she was going to be able to forget what Dad had done. I applauded her for making the best choice for her.

Mom and I were working on our relationship every day, whereas, with my father, I barely saw him and preferred it that way.

Nash slung an arm around Raven and used his fingers to whistle loudly.

I smiled at Amelia and Oliver Beaumont because I was happy they were able to join us and for their presence in my life.

And then there was Easton.

His presence in my life was a story of its own and while we started as a jagged puzzle, we now fit together perfectly. I couldn't believe how his life had become intertwined with mine, even when we'd been in a long-distance relationship for almost the last year or so because Easton graduated last year.

His green eyes met mine and I couldn't help but grin. Even after all this time, when his gaze met mine, it felt as if my heart had stopped beating. How was that fair?

I tore my gaze away, fixing it on the stage ahead. If I looked at him again, I'd trip over my own feet.

After what seemed like hours of talking and clapping, it was nice to collect our diplomas. When the president of our university called my name, the crowd cheered.

I shook the president's hand as I grabbed my diploma. Once I had it and walked across the stage, I was already scanning the crowd for Easton. Our eyes met again, and the world narrowed to just the two of us.

I couldn't wait for all of this to be over so I could be in his arms again.

When the ceremony came to an end, I made my way

through the crowd until I was back to the person I wanted to be around most in the entire world.

"Took you long enough," Easton said when I was inches away from him. He opened his arms up to me. "Thought I might have to charge the stage and carry you off myself."

"In your dreams," I said as I moved into his embrace.

His arms were my happy place. I breathed deeply, the tension draining from my body. This was where I belonged.

"Congratulations, princess." His lips brushed my ear, and I couldn't help but tremble. "You did it."

I smiled against his chest. "You helped me so much, and I greatly appreciate it."

Easton pulled back to meet my gaze, his own softening. "So, you ready for New York?"

"I'm ready to be wherever you are, and if that means moving to New York City where you are right now, then so be it."

His lips crashed into mine, and for a breathless moment, there was only this connection. The tenderness of his kiss and the warmth of his body pressed against mine were all that I could sense and feel. The cheers and whistles of our family and friends faded into the background. There was no crowd, no ceremony, only Easton.

And that's just the way I wanted it to be.

THANK YOU FOR READING! Although Bianca and Easton's trilogy is complete, you can see them in The Westwick University series, starting with The Lies Beneath. Also be sure to check out Aria and Landon's story, The Whispers Below. Keep reading to find a sneak peek of them!

DON'T WANT to let Bianca and Easton go just yet? Click HERE to grab a bonus scene featuring the couple!

WANT to join the discussion about the The Brentson University Series? Click HERE to join my Reader Group on Facebook.

PLEASE JOIN my newsletter to find out the latest about The Brentson University series and my other books!

THE WHISPERS BELOW BLURB

Whispers can be deadly...

In the ancient halls of Westwick University, secrets are currency.

And my objective is to uncover them all.

My mission is to track Aria Townsend's every move.

What makes this situation odd is that she's the sister of one of the most powerful men in the world.

But not only that, her brother is the one that has given me this mission.

I need to find out exactly what she knows and how deeply involved she is in all of this.

Because above all else, I must protect the Chevaliers. No matter the cost.

Sometimes, the truth won't set you free.

The Whispers Below is a standalone dark forbidden college romance that has enemies-to-lovers themes. This book may not be suitable for all readers due to dubious situations that might be triggering. It ends in a happily ever after.

PREVIEW OF THE WHISPERS BELOW
LANDON

It was time.

I drove my black sedan with dark-tinted windows past the gates of Westwick University. I had to admit that my car fit in well here as it was an institution that not only thrived on academics, but the haunted atmosphere that was prevalent here.

It made me think that what I was being sent here to do would be even easier for me to do. There were so many dark corners that I could hide behind and the shadows that surrounded this place would become my best friends.

The assignment I accepted flashed through my mind: Follow Aria, a student at Westwick University who was seen getting close to Iris Bennington. Uncover the truth.

I forced my sedan to a stop in a deserted parking lot. The hum of the engine came to an end as I turned off the engine with the click of a button. Silence surrounded me in this space, and it was heavy and expectant for what lay ahead.

It was time.

I slid out and the blistering cold greeted me as I scanned

the courtyard. A flurry of movement caught my eye, leading my gaze right to her. A girl with long, curly brown hair wearing a blue hoodie with a navy backpack slung casually over one shoulder.

Aria.

I inhaled quickly as she came into view, clearer and clearer with each step. Aria Townsend, Parker Townsend's beloved sister, was the person I was supposed to watch under the guise of me being the newest transfer student to West-wick University.

Our gazes locked across the distance, hazel eyes meeting blue. A jolt shuddered through me as she gave me a friendly smile.

She didn't fucking know what she was getting herself into.

I gave her a smile in return, but I didn't approach. That would happen in due time.

She wanted to play with fire and force her brother to call me in? Fine.

Let the games begin.

The Whispers Below is available for preorder now. It will be released in 2024.

THE LIES BENEATH BLURB

Privilege has its secrets...

Westwick University is known for its prestige and pedigree for hundreds of years.

Many people would die to come here...

And some have come here and died.

There are lies buried within these walls that the world doesn't know about.

But I do.

It's what happens when your family has gone to the same college for generations.

Stories and secrets are passed down, making me yearn to know more.

I'm determined to discover if each and every one is true, but I'm distracted.

Because my new professor has taken a particular interest in me.

Or so I think.

I shouldn't be tempted because anything with him is forbidden.

But the way that he only has eyes for me has set me on edge.

I can't tell if there is something there or if I'm making it all up in my head.

Why would a billionaire, who is known for his solitary life after the death of his wife, want to teach here?

There's so much I don't know.

But I know that lies do nothing but lead to more lies.

And when I uncover the truth, the world will implode.

The Lies Beneath is the first book in a dark forbidden college romance duet that has enemies-to-lovers themes. This book may not be suitable for all readers due to dubious situations that might be triggering. It ends in a cliffhanger.

PREVIEW OF THE LIES BENEATH

IRIS

The loud noises that were coming from the crowd fed into the energy I felt and that wasn't a good thing. This was supposed to be a minor reprieve from my daily routine and wasn't.

I hated being this nervous. This wasn't my scene but stepping outside of my comfort zone was supposed to be a good thing. Here I was at a football game watching my college's team play against our biggest rivals. I eagerly accepted Bianca's invitation to attend because I hadn't seen her in a while. But I didn't come here only to see her and to be mildly entertained for a few hours.

I wanted to get out of my dorm room and to socialize. The eeriness that surrounded Westwick University seemed to stay at the campus's gates and I was grateful. The secrets and darkness that were contained in centuries old architecture hadn't followed me to Brentson's football field. It felt as if a heavy boulder had been lifted off of my chest because I didn't have to worry about *him.*

Sports weren't my thing and me veering away from my

usual haunts should confuse him. Then again, if he was following me like I assumed he was, me changing my schedule slightly wouldn't mean a thing.

It would allow me time away from his gaze that sometimes rendered me useless. Whenever I was on campus, deep down I knew that he was always there, lurking in the shadows, watching every move I made.

As I shifted through the crowd, it was nice to be just one of many. It meant that I could blend in and not be the center of attention. Then again, the purple tips of my hair drew more attention than I'd been accustomed to, but I'd done that for my own benefit and no one else's. If people wanted to stare, then so be it.

Except for when it came to him.

The way he studied me was very measured and what it made me feel was almost indescribable. I was intimidated because I could never tell what he was thinking as he stared at me. It was as if he was undressing me with his eyes, slowly peeling back every layer of clothing until he had me bare.

But it was more than that. I noticed something in his measured approach. It seemed as if he enjoyed making me uncomfortable, but I could prove none of this. Simply staring at someone wasn't a cause for a concern, but it should be when it comes from him.

My professor.

And my boss.

How I ended up being a teaching assistant for him seemed to have happened by chance, but the more things happened, the more I wondered if it truly was a coincidence.

I forced myself to look into the crowd to see if I saw Bianca.

This was the first time in I didn't know how long that I didn't feel as if he was anywhere nearby.

And then it happened. My entire body felt as if it were on edge and that meant only one thing:

He was here.

I could feel his presence in this stadium full of people. That sounded strange, I know, but I also knew what this feeling was. I'd grown accustomed to him being in the same vicinity and the slight shift in air was there.

The coldness in his eyes sent a shiver down my spine even though I hadn't turned around to find out where he was today. No, I wouldn't give him the time of day.

Instead, I saw my friend's profile and walked straight to where she was sitting with another woman.

"Bianca?" I asked although I was pretty certain it was her. When she turned to face me, a wide grin took over her entire face.

"Iris, hey!" Bianca quickly pulled me into her arms before I had a chance to react. When we broke apart, she gestured to the woman standing beside her. "Iris, this is Raven. She's my brother's girlfriend. Raven, this is my friend, Iris."

"It's nice to meet you," I said as we shook hands.

"Likewise," Raven replied. "I'll move down and you can sit on the other side of Bianca."

I'd never heard Bianca mention Raven, but she seemed pretty adamant that we should meet and this was a perfect opportunity to do so.

I could feel him watching my every move as Bianca and Raven moved so that I could take the seat they were saving. As we got settled in our seats, I looked up and saw Raven look behind us and pause. That was when I knew she'd spotted him.

I hated that my instincts were right in this case. I debated saying something, but what was there to say? The professor that I was a teaching aide for was stalking me?

And I knew that he'd killed for me?

No. I couldn't say a word.

The ringing of Bianca's phone snatched our attention and I was relieved. It would save me from having to speak on something that could mean life or death.

The Lies Beneath is available now.

ABOUT THE AUTHOR

Bri loves a good romance, especially ones that involve a hot anti-hero. That is why she likes to turn the dial up a notch with her own writing. Her Broken Cross series is her debut dark romance series.

She spends most of her time hanging out with her family, plotting her next novel, or reading books by other romance authors.

briblackwood.com

ALSO BY BRI BLACKWOOD

Broken Cross Series

Sinners Empire (Prequel)

Savage Empire

Scarred Empire

Steel Empire

Shadow Empire

Secret Empire

Stolen Empire

The Broken Cross Series Box Set: Books 1-3

The Broken Cross Series Box Set: Books 4-6

The Ruthless Billionaire Trilogy

The Billionaire's Auction

The Billionaire's Possession

The Billionaire's Vengeance

Brentson University Series

Devious Game

Devious Secret

Devious Heir

The Westwick University Series

The Lies Beneath

The Truth Between

The Whispers Below

The Shattered Trilogy

Shattered Saint

Shattered Sinner

Shattered Reign

The Devilish Billionaire Series

The Devilish Billionaire: Season 1

The Devilish Billionaire: Season 2